Forbidden Love

Love Stings Series, Book 3

By Evan Grace

Forbidden Love

Copyright © 2017 by Evan Grace.
All rights reserved.
First Print Edition: January 2017

Limitless Publishing, LLC
Kailua, HI 96734
www.limitlesspublishing.com

Formatting: Limitless Publishing

ISBN-13: 978-1-68058-963-4
ISBN-10: 1-68058-963-6

Dedication

To my readers:
Your support and love of my books and these
characters I've created mean a lot to me.

Chapter One

Violet

The apartment that my parents are helping me rent is in front of me, and a sense of excitement runs through me. Last year I stayed in the dorms, and it wasn't bad—it just wasn't good either. My roommate was a party girl, and I was not. My dad about had a nervous breakdown when he found out I was moving into co-ed dorms last year.

My dad is a little on the overprotective side. …Okay, *little* is putting it mildly. My dad would keep me and my sisters locked away if he could. I'm okay with it. I'm a total daddy's girl. He and I have always had a special bond. I'm even going to Tulane to major in architecture and minor in business. My hope is to work alongside my dad and uncles. They run the construction and restoration company that my grandpa and his best friend started a long time ago.

Since I was little, I used to go to work with my dad whenever I could and soak up all of the knowledge I got from watching him work. It was a natural next step to go to his alma mater.

My mom and I climb out of my car, and my dad and uncle climb out of the moving truck.

"I don't like it," I hear my dad say from behind me. "That's it—we're moving you home."

"Daddy, you don't mean that. This is a safe building. You have to buzz to get in."

When I first approached my parents about living off campus, my mom was all for it, but my dad took a little convincing. He only agreed when I let him help me search. We found the perfect spot. I'm five minutes from campus and close to the campus library where I work.

It's a one-bedroom apartment with a tiny eat-in kitchen and a cute little deck that I'll be able to sit out on. We all work together to get my stuff unloaded. My mom and I found the cutest used furniture at a flea market that gives my place a kitschy look, which is just my style. My dad calls me his little hippie chick. My dark hair hangs down to my lower back in wild waves, and I wear a lot of maxi skirts or dresses and bangles on my wrists and ears full of earrings.

Once the last box is brought in, my dad and uncle go to get us pizza, and I sit on my love seat with my mom. "I love this place, Mom. Thank you for all of your help."

She kisses my forehead. "You bet, baby. I hope you have such a good time, but not too good," she says with a goofy smile on her face.

"Please, I'll be too busy studying to have any fun at all. I have Professor Torres for studio work in architectural design. I guess he's really tough and kind of an asshole, but I can handle him. I hope."

"Well, don't let him intimidate you. You're a brilliant girl—a straight-A student and you're an amazing drawer. You get all of that from your daddy, and that's okay because you look just like me."

My dad and uncle return a short time later, and the four of us sit around my living room eating. They're staying the night with me tonight since it's about a ten-hour drive to get home. Since it's only six, my mom and I start unpacking and making up my bed. Uncle Dylan, my dad's twin, and my dad set up my bedroom first. My place is small so it doesn't take long before most of my stuff is up or put away.

I let my parents use my bed with the promise of no monkey business...gross. My uncle blows up the two air mattresses they brought, and I help him make them up. "Thank you for helping today." He flashes me a smile, and it hits me that if I didn't know better, I would think that my dad and uncle were identical twins. They're the only set of fraternal twins I know that look so much alike.

"You're welcome, sweetheart. We're all so proud of you and what you've accomplished. It means so much that you want to follow in your old man's footsteps." I wrap my arms around my uncle, and after I hug him, I head into the bathroom to get ready for bed.

***

I stand on the sidewalk and hug my mom tightly. After going out for breakfast, we came back to my apartment and I listened to my dad and uncle's safety speech. They left mace, a rape whistle, and a blade that looked like a tube of lipstick. I know they mean well and the only reason why they're so overprotective is that my cousin Abby, Uncle Dylan's oldest, was sexually assaulted almost three years ago. It had been bad and then really bad and then better. Now she's married to a gorgeous deputy and the mom to Natalie, Ben's daughter that she officially adopted.

Actually, before I left, they announced that Abby's having a baby. We're all so thrilled for them.

My mom lets me go, and my uncle scoots in front of my dad and scoops me up into a bear hug. "Study hard, no boys." He says the last little bit with a laugh.

"Sure thing. Send my love to Abby, and tell her I expect baby updates." Just the mention of his new grandbaby has him smiling widely.

"You've got it." He kisses her cheek and then helps my mom up into the truck while my dad walks toward me.

"Hey, Daddy." My dad and I have always shared a special bond. Even when I was little, I was attached to his hip. I'm not ashamed at all that I'm a daddy's girl. I've always been able to tell him anything—my hopes, dreams, and fears. He knows that I know about what happened to my mom right before they found out they were having me. I had been doing a family project and found the police reports buried under a bunch of papers. The guy she dated right before Dad turned out to be married, but he was obsessed with my mom and tried to trap her with a baby. He eventually almost killed her but then killed himself.

I started having panic attacks after I found out. Scared that the monster who hurt my mom was actually my father. Dad was great and loaded me up in the car and took me to get a DNA test just so it'd ease my mind, and sure enough, I was 100 percent his kid. We never told Mom because she'd lived through that trauma and I'd never want her to have to relive it.

"Your old man is so proud of you, kiddo. This year is going to be tough, but you've got this. Call me if you have any questions or you just want to talk."

"Thanks, Daddy, you know I will." He gives me a kiss and a hug, and I watch him hop into the truck. I wave to them, and they return it. My mom blows kisses to me as my uncle yells out the window.

"Remember, no boys!"

Laughing, I shake my head. I continue to stand on the sidewalk and watch the truck disappear down the street.

Back inside my apartment, I lock up behind me, look around, and take a deep breath. I head into my room and finish hanging up my clothes. Tomorrow, I start my job in the university library. I like it because I can walk there—it's five minutes from my apartment. It's part of my scholarship to work at the school, and I'll work there three days a week. I also have a job waiting tables at a café on Maple

Street called Organically Delicious.

I'll work there Saturdays and Sundays…so pretty much I'm going to have no life, but that's okay. I didn't have much of one before, either.

After my clothes are in my closet, I grab my stack of textbooks and sit down for some pre-classroom reading.

Chapter Two

Diego

"Come get your stuff. I'm not playing." I'm so angry right now. I can barely see straight.

"Diego, baby. You don't mean that." Penelope's voice comes through the line. She's using that baby sounding voice that she thinks is sexy, but in reality it's grating, and I've never liked it. Hell, I've never really liked *her*. She's hot, sure. She's got a gorgeous body, but she's boring and a bitch. We've only been seeing each other for about four months, but four months too long.

To be honest, I don't know why I even stayed with her. In the beginning I was thinking with my cock, and she could suck it like no other, but no amount of good fucking was going to be able to cancel out everything else that was wrong with her.

"I do mean it," I snarl, "and if you don't get your shit by tonight, then it'll be in a garbage bag on the front steps. Actually, you know what...I'll drop your stuff off at your place." I hang up before she can even respond. In my bedroom, I grab a bra, a bottle of lotion, and magazines that she left at my place. I throw it all in a bag and then grab her toiletries out of my en suite. Shit, I told her not to leave, but of course she didn't listen.

I step outside into the humid, warm air, climb into my Audi A3, and make my way toward Penelope's townhouse. Ten minutes later, I pull up in front of the big white structure that her *daddy* paid for. I do admit that it's a gorgeous home, down in the heart of the Garden District with its white columns, balconies, and wide porch. This is why I chose to teach architecture in New Orleans— beautiful homes, old plantations, and historical structures. I honestly can't wait for school to start next week.

My attention is brought back to the front door as Penelope comes stomping out of her home like a petulant child. A sigh leaves my lips as I grab her bag and climb out of my car.

"Diego, you can't be serious right now." She crosses her arms over her tits and cocks her hip to the side.

I hold out the bag to her. "We are done. I'm tired of your drama."

"Baby, you don't mean that." She comes up to me and trails a finger down my chest. I grab her wrist—not hard, but enough to pull it away from me. "Diego, don't be like this." Her voice is like nails on a chalkboard.

This is the last time I'll let my dick do most of the thinking. No wonder I'm still not married at thirty-four—I have the worst taste in women. *Mi madre* has been telling me this since I first discovered the opposite sex. I admit I've made some shallow choices, choosing women based on their looks. No wonder my longest relationship was only a year. I drop the bag at her feet, step away, and go to my car.

"Diego, don't you dare leave." I don't bother giving her the satisfaction of a reaction. Instead, I ignore her, climb into my car, and pull away. My phone immediately starts ringing, but I ignore it. Hopefully this won't last long—otherwise I'll have to change my number.

***

In a corner booth at the café by my home, I type up the syllabus for my Digital Media I class. I've always loved architecture, but I found that I was a helluva teacher and could teach and mold students into artists. I admit I'm tough on my students, but to pick out the best, I have to be. My reputation as an asshole was well earned because I am one.

I give each of my students the best and expect them to do the same. This year, I've been named head of the architecture department, which is such an amazing honor to me. I've taught here at Tulane for the past four years. In my native Spain, I went to school at Polytechnic University of Catalonia and got my master's in architecture, urbanism, and building construction.

Typing away on my laptop, I take a sip of my coffee and set it back down. My phone vibrates, and I pick it up, rolling my eyes when I see it's

9

Penelope. It's been two days since I brought her things to her, and at least five times a day she texts me. This text is the same as the others.

Penelope: Diego, call me. Come on please.

I don't respond, so a few minutes later my phone vibrates.

Penelope: You're such a fucking asshole! Rot in hell!

"*Folla mi vida,*" I mutter to myself. The only solution for now is to power down my phone. Who knows how much time passes when I hear the jingle of the door opening. My eyes drift toward it, and I'm struck speechless. She is the most exquisite woman I've ever seen.

From here, I can tell she's tall with curves that make me want to grab on. Her sable locks hang down her back in big waves. She's got kissable lips and tits that would make a grown man weep.

She glances in my direction, smiling, and I want to go to her, but I don't. I keep my ass in my chair. I'm seriously attracted to her, so that can only mean one thing—okay, maybe two: she's dumb and a bitch. *Dios,* I sound like an asshole, but history has proven I have shitty taste in women. Back to work I go and force myself to look at my laptop. Ten minutes pass by, and I look up and no longer see the beautiful woman. A sigh leaves my lips as I close up my laptop and pack my stuff away.

I toss a few dollars on the table for the waitress

and make my way out into the warm afternoon. Tomorrow I'm moving into my new office, and I need to check the computers in the lab to make sure they all work. My list for my first class is small, but that's because it's at nine in the morning on a Monday, and usually only the die-hard students sign up for those classes.

In my car, I turn my phone back on, and the notification beep goes crazy. I delete the three texts from Penelope and find a text from my brother, Jorge.

Jorge: Mama told me to text you and let you know that the care package she promised you should be coming Monday or Tuesday.

Jorge is three years older than I am. He's a lawyer and has his own practice in our hometown of Náquera, in Valencian Country.

Diego: Okay thanks. How is Marisol and the kids?

My brother, Mr. Family Man, has a beautiful, sweet wife and four adorable children ranging from ten to three: Jorge Jr., Alejandro, Mariana, and little Sofia. Marisol and Jorge have been together since they were teens, and I'd never admit it to anyone that I've always been a little envious of what they have. Jorge was able to find a woman who is beautiful, smart, and sweet.

Jorge: Fantástico. Junior is a forward on his

fútbol team. Sofia loves watching su hermano play and usually tries to run out on the field to play too.

We talk for a little while longer before he has to let me go due to a meeting. I tell him that I'll watch for my care package and to kiss his wife and babies for me. With a little toss and thud, my phone lands in the passenger seat. I race across town and run into my house to grab my supplies and then carry them out to my car. I might as well set up my office.

I pull into the parking lot by Richardson Hall. It's home to all of the architecture classrooms, labs, and staff. My favorite coffee is served at The Drawing Board, a quaint little café when you first walk in the building. Just a thought of their coffee cake makes my mouth water. They're part of the reason why I exercise so much during the school year. After grabbing my box of supplies, I make my way inside, taking a left. I smile when I see my office straight ahead.

Katherine has been the assistant to the head of the department for the past ten years. She's already sitting behind her desk that is set right outside of my office. As I approach, she looks up and smiles. "Good afternoon, Professor Torres. What are you doing here?"

"*Hola,* Katherine. I've told you to please call me Diego." She nods at me. "I just decided to get a head start on preparing for classes. I also wanted to go up to the lab and make sure everything was working properly."

After putting all of my supplies away, I place my

books on the shelves and then break down the box, sticking it by the door to take home later. My shoes echo on the flooring as I make my way upstairs to my classroom for my design classes. I pull out my keys and unlock the door, flipping the switch as I enter. The scent of different cleansers tickles my nose, but I'm not surprised. The week before classes start they clean the rooms one more time in preparation.

I walk over to my desk and turn my computer on. Once it's booted up, I log in and pull up a design plan. Grabbing the HDMI cable, I make sure that the image appears on the big screen. It does, so I unhook it and shut the computer down. I move around the classroom and boot up each computer; thankfully they're all in working order.

Moving toward the door, I look back one more time at my room. In a few days this room will be full of eager students. Some will make it, and some will fail.

Chapter Three

Violet

Tomorrow, morning classes start, and I'm always a little nervous. Two of my professors I've had before and I know they're great, but it's Professor Torres that makes me nervous. I've heard he's tough and kind of an asshole. I looked him up on the school's website so I know he's cute. Maybe knowing that he looks good will help ease some of the pressure.

My microwave dings so I get up and grab my dinner. Lean Cuisine pepperoni pizza, yum.

I miss my mom's cooking already. Her specialty and my favorite is her *Caruru de Camarao*. It's a Brazilian gumbo with shrimp and okra. My grandma is from just outside of Sao Paulo, Brazil, and taught my mom, me, and my sisters how to cook traditional dishes so we could keep passing them down. I bite into my pizza and savor the flavors. Is it the best I've ever eaten? No, but it'll do until this coming weekend when I can make my

14

gumbo.

My phone rings, and I pick it up to see my dad wants to Facetime me. "Hi, Daddy."

"Hey, my sweet girl. What are you up to?" I can see that my dad's sitting out on the back deck. Probably drinking a beer. For a man in his early fifties, he's still handsome. His hair is dark brown, with some silver throughout. His eyes are the prettiest blue I've ever seen. He's got laugh lines around his mouth and slight crow's feet around his eyes.

"Nothing, just mentally preparing for tomorrow. You know the first day always freaks me out."

"Don't worry yourself too hard. I don't want you to start getting sick again."

I have a bit of an anxiety problem—worrying about everything is what I live with. Sometimes it hits me out of nowhere. Sometimes I can feel it coming on and just do my relaxation techniques. As long as I continue to take my medication every day, the panicky feeling isn't bad.

That's not to say that I don't have bad days, because I do. When it hits bad, I have Ativan, and that helps. I just hate the way I feel after taking it.

"I'm not, I promise. Where are Mom and the girls?"

"Lilah went with your mom to go see your Grandma and Grandpa Hutchins until Daisy finishes at the school." My baby sister is an amazing artist, and at fifteen she's already sold several pieces. She paints and sculpts, and this past year she started blowing glass. The girl is seriously, wickedly talented.

I feel my nose burn and the tears build in my eyes. "I miss you guys." I'm a crier, and I hate it. I cry when I'm happy, mad, sad, and frustrated. People see it as a weakness, which makes me wish it would stop more, but I can't help it. My Grandpa H. told me it's because I'm just passionate and wear my heart on my sleeve.

"Baby girl, don't cry. You know I can't stand it when one of my girls cries." I give him a watery smile. Being in a house with four women couldn't be easy. My sisters and I fight like you would not believe, but we're also really close. Lilah and Daisy have a little bit of a tighter bond, but then again, my dad and I have an extremely close bond.

"Sorry, Daddy. I don't know why I'm crying. It's not like I've never been away from home before."

"Do you need me to fly down there and stay with you for a couple of days?"

My dad would do it, too. He's a wonderful caretaker to us girls and our mom. We're incredibly spoiled.

I wipe the tears from my eyes. "No, I'm okay. It's just a little lonely here without a roommate or Lilah and Daisy always talking my ear off. I'll be okay…just don't tell Mom I was crying. You know she worries."

"Okay, baby girl. You call me day or night if you need me."

I promise him I will and then say goodbye. Placing my phone on the coffee table, I pick up my pizza and finish eating it. After I'm finished, I clean up and do a little bit more reading.

I'm hoping that Professor Torres isn't as bad as they say. He's the only teacher I haven't met yet. I was so upset when I heard Professor Jacobs was leaving so he wouldn't be teaching there this year.

After getting ready for bed, I crawl in between my sheets and turn on my noise machine. Soon the sound of rain lulls me to sleep.

***

I swipe lipstick on my lips. The light wine color looks amazing with my coloring—olive skin with brown eyes and brown hair the color of milk chocolate. My outfit is a peasant dress that comes down to my knees. Under it is a dusty rose-colored slip made of silk; I saw it in a lingerie store and had to have it. A pair of kick ass gladiator sandals with ties that go all the way up to right below my knees grace my feet. Both of my sisters can't believe that I wear skirts and dresses all of the time, but this is what I'm most comfortable in.

My messenger bag is on my little kitchen table. I stuff my laptop in it and have my two textbooks that I'll need today. My dad couldn't believe I picked a class at nine in the morning on a Monday, but I'm not a big partier, so getting up early is easy for me. Plus, my day is done by one o'clock, which means I can do whatever I want for the rest of the day.

I put it across my body and step into the hall, locking my door behind me. Once I'm outside, I slip my sunglasses on and start walking toward campus. It's a quarter after eight, but it's already hot and humid. I stop walking, throw my hair up

17

into a knot on the top of my head, and then begin walking again.

Once I'm on campus, the trees lining the path provide some shelter from the sun beating down on me. Richardson Hall is up ahead, and I feel my stomach start to turn a little bit as nerves take hold. Up at the top of the stairs I step through the door. There are quite a few people around. I recognize a couple of guys I shared classes with and give them a wave when they call out to me.

At The Drawing Board, the coffee house inside Richardson Hall, I order a vanilla latte. I stand to the side and wait for my drink. My eyes move around the coffee shop when I spot Professor Torres. He's sitting in the corner with a cup of coffee in front of him and his face buried in a book. Why are my nipples tingling? He's so much better looking in person. His skin is a shade or two darker than mine. Dark stubble shadows his jaw and gives him a dangerous look.

My name being called pulls me from the trance Professor Torres seems to have over me. I turn back to the counter, hoping no one saw me stare at him. I thank the girl, take my cup, and when I turn around, I see he's gone. Moving around the tables, I take his vacated seat. When I sit down, a woodsy scent wraps around me, and I know whatever it is, the scent is from him. *What is happening to me?* I think. Oh well, it doesn't matter anyway since he's a teacher and I'm a student.

As I sip my latte, I text my mom quickly to let her know I'm going into my first class soon.

Mom: Good luck, my sweet girl. You're going to be amazing!!

Violet: Thanks mama! I love you.

I put my phone on vibrate and stuff it into my messenger bag. Swallowing the last little bit of my drink, I make my way upstairs to the lab where my first class is. The class doesn't start for another fifteen minutes, but I like to be early. After reaching the door, I pull it open and step inside. The only other person in the room is Clint, a guy I met last year. He's very smart, cute in a dorky way, and just different—I can't explain it.

"Hey, Clint. How was your summer?" I grab the seat across from him.

"It was good, Violet. Did you work for your dad?"

"Yeah, I mostly did secretarial work. I did get to watch him work on a couple of plans. He said this next summer he'd let me get more hands-on."

"That's awesome. I'll wait until the end of this semester before I start applying for internships." He never looks me in the eye when he talks to me, and I find it endearing. Clint rubs a hand through his hair and then looks toward the door. "Professor Torres. Hello."

I turn around in my chair and freeze. The beautiful man from the coffee shop is standing just inside the door. Clint stands up, and I follow suit. I don't know why we're standing, but I'm able to size Professor Torres up now. He's taller than I expected, and his body is muscular—his suit is fitted and shows off said body. His hair is a deep, rich brown with the eyebrows to match. He's got a five o'clock shadow already. Professor Torres's suit is a sleek gray with a white dress shirt and a black tie.

"And you are?" His deep voice rumbles with a hint of an accent as he looks at Clint.

"Clint Webster." Clint holds out his hand to Professor Torres. I forgot about how much of a brown-noser he can be. The professor holds out his hand to Clint and gives it a quick shake. He turns to me, and I swear butterflies take flight in my stomach.

At first he doesn't speak—he just stares at me, unblinking, and I hold his stare. He finally blinks, and his face goes blank...weird. "What's your name?"

"Violet Carmichael." I might as well be like Clint, but when I reach out to shake his hand, he looks down at it and then walks away. *What the fuck*, I think as I watch him walk toward his desk.

I look at Clint, and he just shrugs before taking his seat. I sit down and watch Professor Torres set his messenger bag on his desk and begin pulling books and notebooks out of it. The classroom begins to fill up with the other students, and I watch, completely shocked and flabbergasted that the asshole is greeting everyone else. I stare daggers at him, but it's not like the jerk looks at me anyway.

There's only one other girl in here with me, and she's looking at the professor like she wants to eat him.

"Good morning, everyone. I'm Professor Diego

Torres. Welcome to digital media one." He passes out the class syllabus, and then he spends the next ten minutes reviewing it with us.

By the time class is over, I'm ready to be out of this room. We've got reading to do before our next class on Wednesday. I only have two other classes today, and they're pretty much the same—get the syllabus and review it. I've got a lot of reading that I'm going to need to do. After my history and theory of architecture and urbanism, I make my way downstairs to the coffee shop to grab a latte and a sandwich.

I grab a table toward the back and place my bag on top of it. While I eat my sandwich and drink my latte, I read through my textbooks, making notes. I've always been a bit of an overachiever. Always trying to excel at everything I do is my biggest flaw. When I look up, I see Professor Torres standing at the counter but looking at me. I hold the asshole's stare, challenging him to look away. It's only when the blonde girl behind the counter purrs his name that he looks away, but he pays her no attention and then turns back to me.

Whatever. I roll my eyes and look back down at my book and write more notes. I smell him before I see him and look up to find him standing next to my table looking down at me. "Trying to stay on top of your studies?"

He's actually acknowledging me. Wow. "Um, yes. I prefer to stay on top of things."

Professor Torres doesn't say anything—he just watches me with those dark, intense eyes.

"Good," he says, and then he walks away. I stare

after him, wondering what the heck just happened.

***

I'm working on my homework at my kitchen table when my phone beeps at me. I pick it up and see it's a text from my sister, Lilah.

Lilah: Hey sissy, how's school? Have you met any hot guys?

As soon as I read my sister's question, Professor Torres pops into my mind...dammit. It's been two weeks since class started, and so far he's lived up to his reputation as an asshole, which sucks because he's so freaking gorgeous, and when he speaks, his Spanish accent causes tingles up and down my body.

Every time the man asks a question, he wants a ten-minute answer, and then he challenges whatever you say. He and I have already gone head-to-head multiple times. The man is infuriating, and I swear he hates me. Every answer I give he challenges, and I don't know if he's trying to make me feel stupid or what, but I don't like it. I don't like *him*.

Violet: School's good. No, no hot guys yet. How's everyone at home? How's Daisy?

Lilah: We're all good. Care Bear's twins are so cute. Daisy's been helping with them and helping with Natalie. Our sister is the resident babysitter. ☺ I miss you.

Tears immediately fill my eyes. Ugh…I hate being such a crybaby. I'm missing everything. My cousin Luke, Carrington's little brother, goes to school at LSU, so I could hop in my car and be there in two hours if I wanted to spend time with family.

Violet: I miss you too. I'll call you guys this weekend. Maybe we can Facetime. I love you!

After she tells me she loves me too, I put my phone down and go back to studying until I have to go to work at the organic café.

***

"Can I get you anything else?" I ask the two businessmen at one of my tables.

"No, sweetheart. We're good." They dismiss me, and I move around my section checking on my other tables. Everyone is good, so I move to the kitchen.

I order a sandwich and a salad to eat on my break, and while I wait I run some of the dishes through the washer. The café isn't super busy right now, so I move to the front while I wait for my food and talk to Dani, one of the other waitresses. She's a student at Tulane too, and she's an English major.

"Violet, you have such pretty hair," Dani says as she picks up one of my curls. I will admit that I do have pretty awesome hair thanks to my mom.

"Thanks. So how are your classes so far?" I ask.

"They're tough this year. I have two advanced

writing classes and a course in women's literature. What are you studying again?" Dani's got strawberry blonde hair in an adorable pixie cut. She's a few inches shorter than I am and super skinny.

So far she's been the only friend I've made. I've always had a hard time making friends, even when I was little. I'm loyal and am a great friend to the ones I've got, but who am I kidding? Most of my friends are family members. My best friend is my cousin Joe—he's three days older than I am, and we have always been more like siblings. As we got older, we became best friends.

"I'm studying architecture. My plan is to work with my dad and uncles when I graduate."

"Oh...do you have that hot professor that everyone talks about. Um...what's his name?" She taps her lip with her index finger while staring up at the ceiling, like she's trying to think of his name.

"Are you talking about Professor Torres?"

"Oh my God, yes! He's so fine. Are you in any of his classes?" She looks at me expectantly.

"Yeah, I have one of his classes Monday, Wednesday, and Friday mornings."

"Well, what's he like?" She moves closer to me. "Does he have a sexy accent? I heard he does."

"He's kind of an asshole, and it makes it very easy to forget that he's good looking and that his accent is very sexy, but he is. He's an asshole, and I think he hates women." Her eyes widen, but her gaze is focused on something behind me.

My stomach dips as that familiar scent wraps around me. In slow motion, I turn and, sure enough,

Professor Torres is standing on the other side of the counter staring at me with no expression on his face. My face heats up, and my pulse begins to race. What if he kicks me out of his class? "Um-uh...Professor T-Torres. Hello."

"Ms. Carmichael." I think he's going to step away from the counter, but instead he leans in farther. "Monday morning at eight, I expect you in my office." Without a word, he turns and walks out the door.

I turn back to Dani. "How much did he hear?" Panic starts to bubble up inside of me.

"I think everything." She gives me a pitying look.

They call me back to the kitchen to get my food, but suddenly my stomach is too upset for me to eat anything.

Chapter Four

Diego

It's only seven thirty in the morning, and I can't stop watching my office door. Ms. Carmichael won't be in until eight, and that's if she even shows up. I'm not sure why I told her to come to my office. Fuck it, I know why. In just a couple of weeks, I've become infatuated with Violet.

God, even her name makes my dick hard, and that's so fucking wrong. She's my student, and I'm her teacher. It doesn't get much more forbidden than that. I've tried telling myself that she's like every girl I've ever dated: beautiful, but bitchy and not very smart.

She is beautiful too, but that is where the similarities stop. I've watched her interact with the other students, and she's always got a genuine smile on her face when she talks to them. Most of the "boys" in my class watch her with apparent lust in their eyes, but she's oblivious, and I hate it. Her hand is always up when I call on students to answer questions. I love to challenge her because she never backs down. Sometimes I purposely do it just to watch her cheeks flush and her eyes flash with a fire that gets my blood pumping.

I'll never admit it to anyone that I jerked off while looking at some of her pictures on social media the night before. I feel like a *gran perverso*, a big pervert.

Last night Penelope stopped by and refused to leave until I talked to her. It took me threatening to call the police for her to finally go. I shudder to think what will happen if she doesn't finally get the hint. That girl is another reason I should stay away from Violet. It proves I have poor taste in women…obviously.

On my side table are six piles of papers. It's a bullshit project, but it'll get me some time to be near her, even though she thinks I'm an asshole. It's for the best that she hold that opinion of me.

Knock, knock. I turn toward the door and find her standing in the doorway. I don't let her see the pleasure I'm feeling as I take a look at her. She's in another one of her dresses that makes her look like a beautiful free spirit. It's the color mauve with swirls of creams and chocolate browns that hit her mid-thigh. Her hair is down in wild curls that hang down her back. Violet's makeup is light, but her lips are a dusky pink.

I let my asshole mask slip into place. "Ms. Carmichael."

She steps into my office. I can tell her bravado is all an act, but I give her kudos for pretending so well. "Good morning, Professor Torres."

"I've got a job for you if you think you can handle it."

"I can handle anything you throw at me." Ahh...I love this. Her eyes are filled with so much fire I'm surprised there isn't smoke coming out of her ears. Violet's arms are crossed, and it's pushing her breasts out. I tell myself to stop staring before she realizes what I'm staring at.

"Good. I figure that since you think I'm an asshole, you can do some tedious work that I don't want to do." I move over to the stacks of papers. "I need these stapled together. I've got them arranged in order so you just have to grab and staple them. It shouldn't be that hard."

I leave her standing there and move behind my desk to have a seat. A small smile graces my lips when I hear her let out a huffing sound and get to work. I pretend to be looking at my email, but in reality I'm watching her grab the papers and start stapling them together. Her teeth sink into her bottom lip, and all I can think of is biting on that juicy flesh myself. See, I'm a total pervert. My emails pop up so I scan them, slowly. I have no reason to stay in here, but I can't make myself leave.

My watch says that it's only been ten minutes, but it feels like longer. Violet's light, spicy scent wraps around me and has been making me crazy. I stand up and walk around my desk to where she's sitting. "I'm going to grab a coffee. Would you like something?"

Violet stops what she's doing and turns to me. "No, thank you." Dismissing me, she turns back to the papers and begins stapling them together. I make my way downstairs and order a coffee and a muffin. While I wait, I look at my phone and see a text from my mom.

Mama: Hola, mi hijo. Have you received your care package yet?

Diego: Hola. No not yet, but I'll check when I get home. I'm at school now.

Sometimes my mom forgets that there is a time difference. It's three in the afternoon back home.

Mama: Oh my. I've lost my head. Are you still going to come home for winter break?

Diego: Of course mama. My flight's already booked. When we get closer to the date I'll email you my flight information.

Mama: Okay. You're not bringing that horrible woman with you, are you?

My brother and his wife had been in town visiting when I first began seeing Penelope, and of course they hated her on sight. Argh…I was so stupid to keep things going with her. She was awful. Her beauty and the easy pussy she offered up had blinded me. I admit that I have an extremely high sex drive and I'm rather vain. Penelope had suited my needs, and me, but in reality it was just convenient.

Diego: No mama. I broke up with her.

Mama: Thank you Jesus. My prayers have been answered. Now we just need to find you a sweet, suitable woman so you can finally get married and give me some grandbabies.

The barista calls my name, and I send a quick text telling my mom that I'll call her later. I grab my coffee and muffin and head back up to my office.

When I step back inside my office, I find it empty. The only thing that proves that she's been here is Violet's scent and all of the papers stapled and in a neat stack. I set my coffee on my desk and eat part of my muffin before collecting all of my papers and my coffee.

I make my way upstairs, passing students rushing toward their classes. A few female students give me a flirtatious smile, but I just politely nod my head as I pass. It's not lost on me that I'm appealing to the opposite sex, but I have no interest. Of course I should not be showing any interest in Violet, but something is drawing me to the dark-haired, exotic beauty.

Once I reach my classroom and step inside, Violet sits at her desk typing away at her laptop. I can't help but smile to myself when I see her pick up a cup of coffee and take a sip of it all while staring daggers at me. With a smile on my face, I turn toward my computer.

When it's time to start, I stand up. "Good morning, everyone. Today we're going to start CAD—computer aided design. We're going to use this program to create a 2D model. As the semester progresses, you'll be creating a 3D model as part of your final assignment. Now I'm sure you'll all be thrilled to know that next semester when you take the second part of this class, I'll be your professor." A few people chuckle, but I ignore it and move through the room. "We're going to come up with a design plan, and we'll go step-by-step through the entire process. Ms. Carmichael, if you would be so kind and pass out the papers on my desk."

She stares at me with wide eyes, and I know she's plotting my death right now. I force myself to look away and move over to my computer so we can begin.

***

Two weeks have passed, and Violet is becoming even more of an obsession. It's so wrong on so many levels, but I can't help it. Every Monday morning I've been having her come to my office to do menial tasks, giving me the chance to spend time with her. We haven't spoken a lot, but by what little she's shared, she has a huge family, and they're extremely close. I know she's wanted to be an architect since she was little, and her dad went here too. Her plan is to work for him and her uncles when she's done with school.

This past Monday I ordered her a latte and a breakfast sandwich and had them waiting by the papers I needed her to get ready. I could tell she didn't want to take them but instead looked at me hostilely and muttered a "thank you." I would take it, that was for sure, and I watched her while she ate the sandwich and drank her latte.

I wish she'd stop wearing those damn dresses and skirts. I've had to force my body to stop reacting when she comes to class or my office. They always show off her centerfold figure and legs that go on for what looks like miles and miles. Then again, I'd be disappointed if she did stop wearing them.

Penelope finally listened to me and has stopped bothering me…for now.

Since Violet's come into my life, I've had to stave my sexual desires with women I've met at clubs. Of course I've chosen women who look like *her,* but it hasn't helped, not when they're not the one I truly want. I will just keep doing what I have to do to keep myself from crossing a line that should never be crossed. Even though I want to cross it. I want to cross it so bad I can taste it.

A knock on my office door pulls me from my inappropriate thoughts and, speak of the devil, it's the star of all of my fantasies as of late. "Yes, Ms. Carmichael. What can I do for you?"

She walks farther into my office, and I can see the look of determination on her face. "Professor Torres, I'd like to know what I've done to deserve the way you've been treating me." Violet crosses her arms in front of her chest. She's on the defensive right now.

"Why, what do you mean, Ms. Carmichael? I think I've treated you just fine."

Moving until she's right in front of my desk, she stares at me with wide eyes. "Just fine? You challenge every answer I give, even though you know I'm right. You make me come in here early every Monday morning to do bullshit work. If you're trying to break me, it won't work." I can see that her hands are balled up into fists, like she's prepared to strike me. I admire the fact that she's not cowering because I can be intimidating. With slow movements, I stand up.

"I'm not trying to break you. You're one of my brightest students. I challenge you because you don't back down. You give it right back to me. Don't you think that things like that will happen in the real world? It's not all…what's the phrase…'sunshine and roses.' You're a woman in a predominately male career. You need to be tough and stand by your decisions and be able to explain why you want things the way you designed them." She turns to face me fully, but she's still standing defensively. "Even working for your family, you'll still have to prove yourself. Making things easy for you is going to do you no favors. You need a thick skin."

Violet doesn't say anything—she just stares at me with those big brown eyes of hers. I could drown in those chocolate pools. She blinks, breaking the spell she's cast over me.

"Fine. Whatever." She's gone before I can say anything more. My palm itches to go after her and spank her sassy, beautiful ass. With a sigh, I move behind my desk and continue grading papers.

Chapter Five

Violet

I'm so glad I waited until Friday afternoon to confront Professor Asshole. I'll at least have two days before I have to see him again. He'll never know that I sort of appreciate the things he said or the fact that I almost puked all over his desk. I have never stood up to someone the way I stood up to him. I had to take an Ativan when I got back to my apartment.

Now I'm making my way toward Baton Rouge and LSU to see my cousin Luke. I figured Mr. Baseball Star would be too busy for me, but he had the afternoon free. This little over an hour drive is gorgeous, and I've enjoyed the passing landscape and lush greenery. When I get close, I use my Bluetooth speaker to call him and let him know. We decide to meet at a café just off of campus.

Twenty minutes later, I pull into the parking lot of Magpie Café. I climb out of my car, and the humid air immediately coats my skin in a fine sheen of sweat. When I step inside, the smell of coffee wakes my senses. I scan the restaurant and find Luke sitting at a table and shake my head. He's got a couple of waitresses flirting with him. He *is* a good-looking guy. He's tall and lean. His hair is in need of a cut, but it's a dirty blond, and he's got green eyes like his dad.

He sees me and stands up, dismissing the girls who both look at me with distaste. Whatever—I ignore them and rush toward my cousin. "Hey, baseball star!" I throw my arms around him, and he lifts me up off of the ground.

"Hey, princess. Looking good, girl." I sit down across from him and pick up my menu.

"Thanks. How's school going? How are your niece and nephew?"

"School's great. I'm honestly happy to be away from the chaos at home. Between baseball and classes, I'm pretty strapped for time but glad you could meet today. The twins are adorable. It's weird that she's a mom, and now Abby's having a baby too. Everyone is growing up." He pulls out his phone and shows me a couple of pictures of the twins, Shay and Ryder. They are absolutely adorable, and Carrington looks so blissfully happy. They've grown so much since I saw them last.

"I bet your mom is in heaven having the two babies to snuggle. Especially with you so far from home."

"Of course. A mom in her element, that's for sure, and Dad's just as obsessed with the babies. Especially after all of the shit that went down with Care Bear last year."

Last year, Carrington had hid it from everyone that she was working as a stripper when she failed her nursing boards. A whole bunch of shit went down, but in the end it brought her to Damien or David (David is his real name), her husband, and those adorable babies.

Our waitress takes our order, and it grosses me out that she's eye-fucking my cousin right in front of me. When she finally walks away, I look at my cousin with a raised brow. "Do they always flock to you like this?"

"What can I say, the ladies love me."

"Oh, you mean the cleat chasers? Just be careful." I've heard rumors about girls who try getting into the ball players' pants and how nasty they can be.

Luke shakes his head and smiles a smile that I'm sure helps him get into many a girl's panties. "Vi, I'm always careful. What about you? Any boys I need to beat the shit out of for Uncle Dustin?"

"No, not unless you want to beat up one of my professors for me. I don't date, and there are no boys or men, whatever."

My dad is the only one who knows that I'm a virgin. I know it's weird that he knows that, but he's my best friend, and I tell him everything. A part of me has always been a little scared of sex. Maybe it's knowing that someone used sex to try and trap my mom that caused me to wait and wait, and I've never met someone worth giving that part of myself to.

We ate in a companionable silence, and then afterward he gave me a tour of campus and showed me the baseball field. I could only shake my head as girls flocked to him like he was some famous major league ballplayer. The girls, of course, gave me the evil eye until Luke told them that I was his cousin. We ended our time together with a Skype video chat with our Grandma and Grandpa Carmichael.

Now I'm heading toward my apartment. I've got studying to do and a Facetime session with my mom and dad. My mom will want an update on the Professor Torres situation or debacle, as I like to call it. Even after I confronted him about his treatment of me, he still treats me like he hates me and thinks I'm dumb. My mom thinks he's got a thing for me—which is preposterous and wrong on so many levels, even though it gives me a slight thrill—and my dad wants to fly into town and "talk" to him. They're just overprotective of us girls and always have been.

Inside my apartment, I make myself some tea and then hit the books.

***

My mom's beautiful face greets me when I log into my Apple account. "Hi, my beautiful baby. I miss you." We look more like sisters than mother and daughter. Her sable-colored hair is shoulder length and in big curls that frame her face. Chocolate brown, almond-shaped eyes identical to mine and Lilah's.

"Hey, Mommy. I miss you too." I get that burning in my nose because I want to cry. "How is everyone?"

"Everyone is good, honey. Your sisters are chomping at the bit for their turn, but I told them they had to wait until your daddy and I talked to you. How are your classes?"

"They're all going well. I'm glad I chose the courses I did. They're tough, but I'm going to learn a lot. How's the studio?"

My mom is a photographer. She does wedding, family, and baby photos. She's so talented and has taken all of our pictures for as long as I can remember. Her camera always seems to be in her hands.

"The studio is good. I just did Care Bear's twins' pictures. They were so good, and the pictures turned out great. I've got a couple of weddings coming up and some senior pictures to do." My mom looks behind her like she's looking for someone and then turns back to me, leaning toward her camera and appearing close up on my laptop screen. "So...are there any guys that you're interested in? Have you been asked out?"

"No, no boys, or men...whatever. I just don't have time. Between school and work, I don't really have a lot of time to worry about boys."

"Thank God for that." My dad's face appears next to my mom's. "No asshole is good enough for my baby girl."

My mom smacks his chest, but then he grabs her and kisses her lips hard. They've never shied away from showing affection toward each other. "Ugh...Daddy, quit mauling Mom." Maybe I wouldn't be so scared of being intimate with a man if I could find someone who looked at me the way my dad looks at my mom.

"Classes going good?" he asks.

"Yeah, I'm really loving CAD. It's amazing what programs are out there right now. We're getting ready to start AutoCAD, and I'm super excited about it." I've always loved working with computers.

"That's great, Vi. When you're home for winter break, you can come to the office with me and show me what you've learned. We'll put it toward your internship hours. Everything else good?"

"Yeah, everything else is good. I made a friend at the café. She's an English major, and her name is Dani. She's super nice, and we might actually meet for a drink tonight." That's a total lie, but my parents are always on me to get out more and act like a typical twenty-one-year-old. The truth is, I'm a homebody and would rather snuggle up on the sofa with a movie and some ice cream than go to a noisy bar where guys are in your face and girls practically fight each other for the attention of some guy who was going to sleep with them and then never call them again. No thank you.

"That's great, sweetheart. We just want you to have fun while you're there and make some lifelong friends." This comes from my mom.

"Just don't have too much fun," my dad pipes in, and I just shake my head. My Uncle Dylan always teases my dad, who used to be a total playboy—ew gross—and karma was funny and gave him three daughters. My dad loves it, though. We all take care of him and spoil him, but in turn he spoils all of us. When I watch my parents together, I know that's

39

the kind of relationship I want. Sure they fight sometimes, but they also love each other fiercely.

I talk to them for a little bit longer and then talk to both of my sisters. Lilah and I look like we could be twins, and Daisy is the female version of our dad. We've always been close even though personality wise we're all three so different. We disconnect a few minutes later, and I'm proud to say that I don't cry, but I am homesick. I decide quickly to call my Grandpa Hutchins; he's my mom's dad.

"Well, hello there, my beautiful girl. How's my oldest granddaughter?"

"Hi, Gramps. I'm good. I just got done talking to Mom and Dad and the girls. How's Grandma?"

"Your grandma is great. It's a hard job keeping me in line," he says with a laugh. "How's school?"

"It's great, and it's going to be a tough year, but I'm excited to learn more."

"Well, I'm sure you're going to ace every class. Baby girl, you helped design the treehouse in our backyard that's still just as sturdy today as the day we built it." When I was sixteen, my dad, grandpa, and I designed and built a huge treehouse. People just assume that since I like to build things that I'm a tomboy. I'm not—I'm just a girly-girl that likes to build stuff.

"I do rock, don't I?" I look at my phone and know I should get back to working on homework. "I hate to cut our conversation short, but I've got some homework to do and have to work in the morning, so it'll be an early night. I love you, and send my love to Grandma."

"Love you too, sweet girl. I'm so proud of you.

You know I love all of you girls, but you and I have a special relationship that I'm very thankful for." Tears cloud my vision. "I see so many great things for you in the future. I can't wait to see you at winter break. I love you, beautiful girl."

"I love you too, Gramps. We'll talk soon." I hang up and look at the picture of my grandpa and me that's hanging on the wall. It was taken the day my mom and dad got married. I'm in his arms in a frilly off-white dress that was identical to my mom's. I've got both hands on his cheeks, and he's smiling widely at me, with my smile just as wide. I shake off the sadness and the homesickness that I'm feeling and get to work on my studies.

***

I stop in The Drawing Board and order a latte for me, a coffee for Professor Torres, and two muffins and make my way toward his office. His assistant isn't here yet, but I still make my way into his office, setting his coffee and muffin on his desk. I inhale my muffin before I begin the arduous—of course I'm being sarcastic—task of stapling papers together.

The quiet is soothing as I work. I can hurry up and get this stuff done and get up to the classroom, avoiding Professor Torres at all costs, which makes no sense since I just bought the man coffee. "It appears we had the same thoughts." I turn to find him stepping into his office.

Why couldn't he be hideous? Maybe have a few warts or a hook nose? Instead he comes walking in like he's ready to pose for *GQ*. His intoxicating scent fills my senses as he steps up behind me and sets my drink on the table. I feel my body lock. Did his chest just brush against my back? His hand appears in front of me with a cherry croissant. I take it and turn around so we're almost touching. I want to reach out and feel the stubble of his cheeks on the palm of my hand. Instead, I hold up the croissant and tell him, "Thank you."

He nods his head before moving to sit down behind his desk. I watch as he sets the coffee he bought down and picks up the one I bought him, taking a generous sip. Quickly looking away, I start separating papers as I listen to Professor Torres tap away on his keyboard. I want to ask him how long he's going to make me do this for, but I don't.

After finishing up with the papers, I dismiss myself, head out of his office, give a quick "hello" to Professor Torres's secretary, and make my way down the hall when a hand suddenly wraps around my forearm. I freeze and find the dickhead. "Yes?" My voice is laced with apparent irritation.

His brown eyes suck me into their depths, and I ignore the warmth that spreads across my lower belly or the fact that I shiver when his hand squeezes my bicep with just enough pressure to stop me from pulling away. "Have you thought about the things I said?"

For a second I forget what he's talking about, and then the day I confronted him pops back into my mind. "Maybe. Why?"

"Maybe because I'm still going to be hard on you and challenge you. If you can handle it, you're going to be very successful."

Great, so he doesn't plan on lightening up on me. "So what? I'm supposed to thank you? Be forever grateful for the 'lessons' you're giving me?"

He leans in close. *"Me encantaría ponerle sobre mi rodilla y azotar su culo, mi espíritu hermoso."*

Before I can reply, he's back down the hall. I'm dizzy all of a sudden; I feel flushed, and my panties are embarrassingly damp. It takes a few seconds for the fog to clear from my brain. Disgusted with myself, I hustle to class.

***

"Yes, Ms. Carmichael?" Professor Torres walks toward me with that cocky swagger of his.

"I just wanted you to take a look at this. What do you think? I went wrong somewhere, and I can't figure it out." He leans down, looking at my screen. I stare blankly at it, trying to control myself as his woodsy scent wraps itself around me.

"Ahh...I see it." He points to the point where two lines meet. "Right here, the lines don't quite touch. It's an easy miscalculation, but in 2D drafting they have to meet or else they could lead to a misrepresentation of your model."

I'm a little stunned right now that he's being so helpful and bordering on being supportive. He shows me a couple of tips, and I thank him before he stands up straight and walks away.

After the class finishes, I pack up my stuff and sling my messenger bag across my body. I feel eyes on my back and turn toward Professor Torres's desk

43

to find him staring at me. His eyes darken, or at least in my mind I believe they are. His stare is unwavering, and I don't dare look away. I'll never give him the power of intimidation over me.

Our battle of wills lasts what feels like a while. It's not until there's a knock on the door that the spell is finally broken between us both. I hustle out of the room like my ass is on fire, embarrassed that the infuriating man turns me into a horny idiot. How the hell can I get horny when I've never had sex before?

I plan on burying my head in my books—that's the perfect distraction.

The rest of my day passes quickly, and before I know it, I'm racing across campus to the library for the few hours I work. I pull open the door and run up the marble stairs until I reach the main desk. "Hi, Patty," I call out as I pass the head librarian.

"Hi, Vi," she hollers out to me.

Once in the break room, I set my bag down and put my hair up in a knot on top of my head. I move back toward the front, grab an empty cart, and pull books out of the return bin. One by one, I check them in and then put them into alphabetical order. After that is done, I move through the library putting the books away. I love that it's a mixture of books—some romance, some mysteries, and some academic.

Once that's done, I move through the tables to straighten the chairs and pick up any garbage left lying around because people were too lazy. In the back, I grab the cleanser and start spraying the tables and vigorously wiping them down. By the time all of my work is done, I head toward the front and grab more books out of the return.

When it's quitting time, I grab my bag out of the back and make my way toward home. I'm starving, so I begin to mentally scan my refrigerator, but I think it's pretty sparse. If so, I'll just head to the grocery store.

By the time I'm stepping into my apartment, my body is covered in a fine sheen of sweat. I turn down the thermostat and move to stand right in front of the register, letting the cool air work its magic on my sweaty body. Once I'm feeling less like a sweaty pig, I flop down onto my sofa and pick up the remote. I haven't done any Netflix binging in a while, so I pull it up and begin the fourth season of *The Gilmore Girls*. Rory reminds me of my sister Daisy, except where Rory has major book smarts, Daisy is an artistic genius…well, she's *our* artistic genius.

I snuggle into the sofa as I get lost in my show. I forget about eating, and it isn't long before my eyes drift shut.

Chapter Six

Diego

I look over everybody's plans, and I'm quite impressed. Everyone got to choose his or her own designs. There are houses, restaurants, stores, and one library. I don't know whose is whose as I look them over and grade them. I'll put the grades on them, and my students will come up and grab theirs—then I'll know who did what. For four of the designs, I've requested to speak to the students who did them. Either I've got a couple of accelerated students, or they cheated, had help, or used someone else's design. I really hope it's the former not the latter.

Out of the three classes I teach of Digital Media I, I'm surprised I don't need to speak to more. Looking at my computer, I see it's almost time for my morning class to begin. I throw the designs from that class into my bag and make my way upstairs. I'm so glad it's Friday. It's been a brutal week, and I honestly just need to decompress. Tonight I need to go out and scratch my itch because my hand and thoughts of Violet are not helping the constant need that fills my body.

Fuck, now my cock is hard. I've got serious problems. Not only am I too old for her, but I'm her teacher, and it could mean the end of my career as well as get her kicked out of school. But why does the thought of burying myself in her tight, hot pussy make it almost worth it? I could just image her lying across my desk, like a feast spread before me. Is she shaved or is she au naturale? Does she taste as good as she smells?

I rub my aching cock through my pants and try to get myself under control. See? I need to fuck, and I need to fuck a lot to get these feelings for her to go away. Now I know what drug addicts feel like, except for the fact that I haven't even fucked her so I have nothing to compare it to.

Once my dick calms itself, I make my way up to my class. I purposely arrive a few minutes late to get everyone on edge. They all stare at me when I walk in, but I don't let on that I even realize I'm late. I hang my bag on the back of the chair and grab the designs out of it. I spread them out on the table.

"Okay, everyone—here are your designs. Please come and grab yours. Now remember, I don't know whose was whose, and there are notes on the bottom. Read over them closely, and if need be, we can arrange some office time to go over them."

One by one, they step up to my desk and look through the papers to grab theirs. I watch Violet as she makes her way up to my desk. I'm shocked as she grabs the library design. It's by far the best design that I've seen, but it's also one I suspect that the person got help with. I watch as she reads my comments at the bottom. ***"Please see me in my office after class to discuss your design"*** is what it says, and her eyes widen as she looks up at me. I keep my face neutral and don't give anything away.

I'm slightly disappointed that someone helped her with her design. With a sigh, I start our lesson for today.

***

A knock on my office door has me looking up to find Violet standing there. "Come in and please shut the door." She does and then sits down on the other side of my desk. "Ms. Carmichael, I asked you to come meet me to discuss your design. I'd like you to answer me honestly. Who helped you?" There was no reason to beat around the bush.

"What do you mean, who helped me? No one did." I see that familiar spark in her eyes. "Do you really think I'd turn in something that I honestly didn't do by myself?"

"Well, Ms. Carmichael, people will sometimes do anything to make themselves look good."

Violet pushes herself up until she's standing and slaps her hands on my desk. "Are you kidding me right now? I did that design all by myself. How dare you accuse me of having someone help me? I'll show you right now that I did it alone." She grabs her laptop out of her bag and slaps it on my desk.

I watch in stunned silence as she pulls up a

program on her laptop and starts tapping away on her keyboard. She stops and picks it up, coming around to my side, and I watch as she works with a speed that seriously impresses me. It's very obvious that I've made a mistake here. Violet knows what she's doing and is confident in her work. Before I can stop myself, I reach out and place my hand on her arm to stop her typing.

"Why'd you stop me?" she asks as I stand up. We're so close we're almost touching. This close to her, I can see the gold flecks in her eyes.

"I believe you. I'm sorry I thought you had help. Yours was the best I've seen in a long time." I warm inside when I watch a touch of pink bloom on her cheeks. "You're extremely gifted." I feel myself lean toward her and feel her lean toward me. It's like we're two magnets, and the pull is intense. I've never in my life felt this kind of pull toward someone. If I'm being honest, it freaks me out just a little. Right now I'd give my left nut to be able to mark her, to taste her.

My office phone ringing breaks the spell, and we both lean back. Violet doesn't say a word—she just stares at me with those hypnotic eyes of hers. The phone stops ringing, but I don't care.

She finally speaks. "Um...th-thank you for believing me. I should probably go."

Violet's gone before I can even stop her. I walk over and lock the door for privacy and then sit down at my desk. I undo my pants and pull my hard, aching cock out. My imagination conjures up the perfect scene in my head. Violet is between my legs with her lips wrapped around my cock. I stroke my dick as I imagine it's her hand wrapped around the base of my aching member as her mouth works its magic.

In my head, I can hear her moans as she sucks my cock into the back of her throat. It takes only a few strokes before I'm moaning and spraying my cum into a tissue. "Jesus," I mutter to myself. I've honestly never come that hard before. It takes me a few minutes to get myself tucked back in and cleaned up. I need to get myself under control before I throw my career down the toilet all for some forbidden pussy.

***

The bass moves through me as I step into the Furry Pussy. It's the most God-awful name for a club, but it's a great place to pick up a beautiful woman. It takes a few seconds for my eyes to adjust to the dark room. The dance floor is packed, and there are women everywhere. I scan the crowd to see if there are any women that pique my interest. My eyes catch sight of a woman that gets my dick stirring in my pants.

Her dark hair hangs down her back in sleek strands. From where I am, her body appears to be curvy in all of the right spots. I want to see her face. I need to see her face. If her front is as hot as her back, then I'm in for a good time tonight.

My eyes burn into her backside as I watch her sway to the music. I want to fit my front against her back while I grind my hard dick against her.

When she finally turns around, I feel like

someone is trying to mess with me. Violet's body moves seductively as she faces me. I know she doesn't see me, so I move toward the darkened corner so I can watch her without being seen. She's dancing with the girl from the café. I'm not the only one watching her, but I can't blame the others. Violet looks like sex on a stick. Her dress is so short that I'm surprised I can't see ass cheeks.

It's taking everything I have not to go to her. Women are everywhere, but I don't see them. How could any of them compare to her? They can't, so instead of taking a girl home tonight, I'm taking myself home to jerk off and think about Violet. If I can't get myself under control when it comes to her, then I'm going to have to come up with some sort of plan.

I make my way back toward my home and jerk off until I can't anymore.

***

This has been the Monday from hell, and it's only eight in the morning. First, I overslept. Second, I spilled my coffee all over myself and my tiled kitchen floor. Third, my pants got snagged when I ran into my door.

I park my car in the staff parking lot and move quickly toward the building. My plan is to dismiss Violet as soon as I step into my office. I need to quit being alone with her because all it's making me want to do is cross that forbidden line. Maybe that's why I'm cranky, because I don't want to do it.

Wrapped up in my work, I don't even realize that

Violet didn't show up until my assistant pokes her head in asking if I was going to class. Now I'm jogging up the stairs to my classroom. I'm ten minutes late. Just outside the door, I take a deep breath and hope that the class goes well.

"I'm sorry I'm so late. It won't happen again." I set my bag on my desk, pull out the handouts, and begin passing them out. Of course they're not stapled together because Violet didn't show up and I lost track of time. I hear a phone vibrate and look around. That is one of my rules: No cellphones or I take them. I continue to hand out the papers when I hear the phone vibrate again.

This may work in my favor when I see Violet look at her phone. I move until I'm standing over Violet. "Answer it, Ms. Carmichael. It must be important if they wish to bother you while you're in my class. Oh, and please put it on speakerphone so we can hear what's so important." With my arms crossed over my chest, I wait for her to answer.

"H-Hey, Dad. What's up?" Her voice shakes a little as her eyes flit to mine.

"Baby girl. I hate doing this over the phone, but your Grandpa Hutchins had a massive heart attack last night." There's a pregnant pause, and then he clears his throat. "Baby, he's gone. I'm so sorry, honey."

My stomach drops, and I feel sick right now. Violet's face visibly pales, and I want to reach out and comfort her, but I don't.

"No, Daddy," she moans. "How's G-Grandma?" Her voice sounds pained, and it's breaking my heart.

"Your mom's there now. I'm booking your flight, and I'll email you the info. How soon can you come?"

Violet pushes back in her chair and stands up. Her eyes are bright with unshed tears as she stares at me like I'm scum, but honestly I *feel* like scum. I open my mouth to tell her I'm sorry, but she holds up her hand. "I don't want to hear anything you have to say. When I get back, I'm dropping this fucking class!" She grabs her bag and storms out of the room while I hear her dad calling her name on speakerphone.

Everyone stares at me, and I feel myself shrink under their scrutiny. I've never not felt confident, but right now I want to just walk out and go to her. I need to apologize, grovel, or beg her not to quit my class, but I can't right now. I'll figure out how to make it up to her.

"All right, everyone, let's get to work."

Chapter Seven

Violet

The plane begins to taxi toward the gate, and I can't wait to be off of it. I throw an Ativan in my mouth and swallow it with the little bit of water that's left in my bottle. I've been on autopilot since my dad called earlier this morning. My heart is utterly broken, but I can't seem to cry. Maybe it's because I need to be strong for my grandma, mom, and sisters. They're going to need me, so I need to make sure that I stay strong for them. I can't afford to lose it now.

I grab my bag from under the seat in front of me and place it in my lap. The seatbelt sign goes off, and I stand up, waiting impatiently as people start moving toward the aisle and then slowly toward the exit. I shuffle along until the crowd thins out and then race-walk toward baggage claim.

I spot my cousin Joe up ahead, but he's hard to miss. He's got to be at least six-foot-three or four. He's muscled but compact. Joe looks a lot like my dad and Uncle Dylan, with the same dark hair sticking out from under the baseball cap he's wearing. His bright blue eyes match theirs, and he's got the same cocky smile. He's a total player, but I love the meathead.

"Hey, handsome." I throw my arms around him, hugging him tight.

"Hey girl, it's good to see you. Sorry about Gary. Your grandpa was a good man." Joe grabs my garment bag and slings it over his shoulder. We make our way outside to his classic black Mustang.

The drive to Beaufort takes us about an hour, and we spend that hour catching up on each other's lives. I'm kind of shocked when Joe tells me that he's going into law enforcement. It was always assumed that he'd go into the construction business like our dads. "What do Aunt JoJo and Uncle Dylan think? What made you change your plans?"

"They're supportive and just want me to do what makes me happy. I guess with everything that's happened between Abby and Carrington, law enforcement just makes sense. I've talked to Ben a lot about it, and the more I talk to him, the more I know it's the right decision." Ben is Abby's husband and Joe's brother-in-law. He just recently started working for the Beaufort Police Department after being a deputy with the Beaufort County Sherriff's Department.

"Well I think it's great, and I think you'll be amazing. Have you been to my house?"

"Yeah, I was there earlier with my parents and Haddie."

I almost don't want to ask Joe my question, but I

do anyway. "How's my mom?"

He glances at me and then at the road. "She was really quiet. She kind of looked spaced out. Lilah and Daisy are doing okay, but they want their big sister."

We pull up in front of my parents' house. The driveway is full of cars. My family is big and loud, but we're always there for each other when we need it. Joe climbs out and grabs my bag for me, meeting me at the driveway. When I reach the front porch, the door flies open, and my cousin Chloe is standing there with her younger brother Carter behind her.

They're the adopted kids of my grandpa's baby brother—my Uncle Garrett and his husband, Ian. They both have hair so dark it's almost black and cerulean blue eyes. Their skin is like porcelain, but a lot of Carter's body is covered in beautiful, colorful tattoos. The two of them are gorgeous and some of the sweetest people I've ever known.

"Vi." Chloe smiles as she rushes toward me and then wraps me in a hug. "I've missed you. You look beautiful."

"Thanks, Chlo. I'm sorry we're seeing each other under these circumstances." Carter hugs me next. He doesn't talk a whole lot, but he always seems to be taking everything in.

I follow Carter to the door, and when I turn around to see if Chloe and Joe are following us, I find them staring at one another with a very heated look. Do I call out to them, or do I just leave them? I decide to do the latter, and I'll just have to grill Chloe later.

Once inside, I spot my mom standing in the

middle of the living room. My dad has his arms around her. I can hear her cries and rush toward her.

My dad turns her in his arms so she's facing me. "Mommy." I wrap my arms around her, holding her tight as she cries into my hair. "I'm so sorry." What more could I say?

"He loved you s-so much." Her voice cracks.

"Come on, Mommy—let's go lie down." I look at my dad, and he nods his head at me. I lead her back to their bedroom. "Where's Grandma?"

"She's asleep in your room. Is that okay? She wanted to wait up for you, but we gave her something so she could sleep. You can sleep in Daisy's room."

In my parents' bedroom, I kick off my shoes and follow my mom onto their bed. My mom wraps her arms around me, and we snuggle until she finally falls asleep. I slowly inch my way out of the bed and silently walk out into the hall to find my dad leaning against the wall. "Hi, Daddy." I walk right into his arms. My eyes burn, and my nose stings but no tears fall.

"I'm so glad you're home. I wanted to come get you, but your mom and sisters were all having a hard time." My dad leads me into the dining room. I can see Carter, Chloe, Joe, and my Aunt JoJo all standing on the deck talking, and we go out to join them.

My aunt and Joe left a while ago, and Chloe and Carter went to stay at my grandma's house, but they promised they'd be back in the morning. The rest of my mom's family is showing up tomorrow. I make myself a cup of tea and take it back out onto the back deck so I can stare out into the night.

This morning comes back to me, and I feel that anger coiled up tight in my belly. I've never been more humiliated in my life. I meant what I said to Professor Torres about dropping his class. Maybe I'll file a complaint against him and then they'll get rid of his arrogant ass. My dad interrupts my thoughts when he steps onto the deck with me. His arm wraps around my shoulders, and I lean into his side.

"You want to tell me what was going on when I called this morning?"

I should tell him, but knowing how protective my dad is, he'd probably show up at school and do something to get me thrown out. "No, it was nothing that I can't handle."

"You'd tell me if you couldn't handle it, right?"

"Yeah, Dad, I would."

He kisses my forehead. "Don't stay up too late. I'll see you in the morning."

I watch him disappear back inside and turn to look out over the backyard. With a sigh, I close my eyes and tilt my head back. A little prayer to stay strong tomorrow and for my anxiety to stay away leaves my lips before I drink down the rest of my tea.

After going through my bedtime routine, I quietly open the door to Daisy's room and step inside. My dad blew up the air mattress earlier for me. Crawling onto it, I stare up at my baby sister, who sleeps peacefully in her bed with her hands tucked up under her chin. With the blanket tucked up under my chin, I let my eyes drift shut.

I slip on my black wrap dress and step in front of the full-length mirror in my mom's room. The sleeves are capped, and it hugs me and then flares out a little at the hips. I keep my makeup light and wear wine-colored lip gloss on my lips. Sitting on the bed, I slide my feet into my black high-heeled strappy sandals.

Yesterday had been the visitation. Grandpa's brothers and my great-grandma showed up the day after I did. She looked so sad when she stepped into my parents' house. My dad, mom, and uncles Garrett and Ian had been at the funeral home finalizing plans when the rest of the family got there. My sisters and I made snacks for everyone and made sure they were all comfortable.

They all wanted to hear about our schooling. Lilah's going to school to learn how to do hair, and Daisy, who just turned sixteen, is still going to high school but doing some art classes at the community college.

The aunts all helped start dinner, and once the rest of my family was back, it was mass chaos. Between stories being told and tears being shed by everyone, it was obvious my grandpa was loved. He worked for the city until he retired a few years ago and loved playing guitar. When we would have dinner at their house, he always busted it out, and while my mom sang and he played, us girls would dance around.

The previous night at the visitation when my mom, uncles, grandma, and great-grandma went in to view the body, their cries could be heard from behind the door. I hugged Daisy as she cried. Carter had his arms wrapped around his sister, and Uncle Ian was hugging Lilah. When we finally stepped into the room, my heart completely shattered watching my mom cry for her dad. She was so inconsolable that my dad had to lead her out of the room until he got her calmed down.

We all had to be strong for her while we stood in the receiving line. My grandpa was loved by a lot of people.

Now, I make my way into the kitchen and find my dad and Lilah leaning against the counter drinking coffee. "Hey guys. Lah, you look beautiful. Daddy, you're very handsome." I kiss both of their cheeks and grab a cup and pour myself coffee.

"Baby girl, you look beautiful. How'd you sleep?" my dad asks as I top off his coffee.

"Okay. Someone came in and wanted to snuggle." I look pointedly at my sister.

Lilah sticks her tongue out at me. "Whatever. *You're* the one who talked my ear off about that asshole professor of yours. If I didn't know better, I'd say you had the hots for him."

I give her a stern look, hoping that Lilah will drop it and the conversation will be over, but no such luck.

"What's going on with your professor, Violet? Is he giving you trouble?" my dad asks over the top of his coffee cup.

"No. He's just tough and kind of an asshole."

"Well, *do* you have the hots for him?" my dad

grumbles.

My sister is going to get it. "No, I don't. Lilah must've misheard me."

Luck is on my side, and I don't have to discuss this ridiculousness anymore because my mom and baby sister step into the kitchen. All four of us girls start to laugh because we're dressed almost exactly the same. My mom and Daisy have their hair up in chignons, and Lilah and I are wearing our hair down, but we're all in black wrap dresses and black high-heeled sandals.

"How did I get so lucky to have so many beautiful women in my life?" Dad says before wrapping his arms around my mom.

After we finish our coffees and have a quick bite, we all make our way toward the church.

We step inside the church, and I can already see people seated inside. The rest of our family on Dad's side is standing in the vestibule talking. Joe comes to me immediately, wrapping his strong arms around me. "How you doing?" he whispers.

I look into his eyes and whisper back, "I'm numb." He kisses my forehead before hugging me again. He steps away, and I make my way toward my grandma, wrapping my arms around her when I reach her. She squeezes my arms and kisses my cheek. Slowly, we make our way inside the sanctuary. My eyes scan the people that are already seated in the pews. We're halfway up the center aisle when a man sitting alone turns toward us, and I see that it's Professor Torres. How did he find out where the funeral was? He probably looked it up online…asshole.

I trip over my own feet but stop myself from falling. "Are you okay?" my grandma whispers to me, and in my extreme embarrassment, I nod and take my seat.

***

While I sip my glass of wine, I watch my uncles, Carter, and Chloe set up their instruments. We decided to have the luncheon/party at my grandma's house so right now there are people milling around, talking and laughing. I want to scream at them to stop being happy, that a wonderful man is gone and now isn't the time to celebrate. Instead, I drink my wine down and go pour myself another glass, chugging it down as well. I hardly ever drink, and I can already feel the effect of the alcohol.

Professor Torres showed up about thirty minutes ago, but I refuse to speak to the prick, and I make sure that I'm always in the opposite part of the house from where he is. The sound of acoustic guitars fills up the house, and then Chloe's hypnotic voice follows. My eyes move toward the flat screen TV that has a video playing—it's showing pictures of my family. My nose burns as I stare at it. Picture after picture flashes up on the screen, and paired with Chloe's singing, I feel my heart start to race and my eyes begin to burn.

A picture I forgot was taken pops up. It's of me, Dad, and Grandpa in this very backyard building the treehouse. I'm between the two of them and smiling widely at the camera with a purple hard hat on my head. Both men smile down at me with so much love and pride on their faces it makes my chest feel tight.

I hustle into the kitchen, thankful to find it empty, and grab a bottle of wine out of the refrigerator, one of my great-uncle's packs of cigarettes, and a lighter, slipping out of the back door. With careful movements, I climb up the ladder and into the treehouse. It's so clean in here, but I know my grandpa would come out there and take care of it. I sit in front of the window and put a cigarette between my lips. I smoked for six months my freshman year of college but then quit when I got bronchitis.

The cigarette dangles from my lips as I light it and inhale that familiar smoky flavor. The music from the house drifts through the open windows and into the backyard. The familiar notes of Grandpa's favorite song, "Everlong" by The Foo Fighters, carry through it, and memories begin to assail me— Grandpa helping teach me how to ride a bike; my sisters and I putting on a recital for Grandma and Grandpa at their home when we'd sleep over; my grandpa pulling me aside at my graduation party and telling me how proud he was of me and that he expected great things from me. He then shocked the shit out of me by handing me a check for fifteen thousand dollars, which I used toward school.

I take a drag from my cigarette, and as I blow it out, the tears begin to fall out of nowhere, and it's like the dam has broken and I can't stop it. I hold the wine bottle up to my lips, taking a generous sip and then setting it down on the floor. As my cries fill the treehouse, a noise has me looking up to find

Professor Torres climbing inside.

"What are you doing here?" I ask as I wipe the tears from my eyes.

He sits down next to me. That familiar woodsy scent of his wraps around me, and I find it weirdly comforting. "I hope it's okay that I'm here. I looked up the information on the internet. I wanted to come and pay my respects, and I wanted to apologize for what happened in class on Monday." Again, he surprises me by grabbing my hand, and with his free hand he grabs my cigarette and stubs it out before tossing it out the window. "Come here." He pulls me to him and wraps his arms around me, hugging me tight. The tears start to flow again as I cry into his neck.

Professor Torres strokes my hair and whispers to me in Spanish. I've got no clue what he's saying, but the words feel sweet and soothing. When my tears finally stop, at least for the time being, I pull away so I can wipe my eyes, but he gets to me first with a handkerchief in his hand. With a gentle touch, he wipes the tears away. The tenderness is unnerving, but I don't want him to stop. Of course now I'm even more emotional, and tears again start leaking.

"T-Thank you for c-coming." I grab the wine bottle and tip it to my lips, taking another generous sip. "Drink?" I hold the bottle up to him and watch as he takes it, tipping it back. A strong desire to lean forward and lick his neck assails me, but I stay strong and don't. He takes another drink before grabbing the pack of cigarettes, shaking one out, and lighting it.

"These aren't good for you," he says with the cigarette between his lips.

I can't pull my eyes away from Professor Torres's lips as he takes a drag and then blows out smoke rings. He hands me the cigarette, and I take a drag while watching him look around the inside of the treehouse. "You helped design and build this?" he asks.

"Yep, when I was sixteen. We worked on it for two solid weeks." I take a drag from the cigarette and pass it to him so he can do the same. "I even broke my finger a week in, but I refused to quit until it was done." I take a drink of the wine. "When we finished, the three of us spent the night up here, eating junk food, drinking soda, and making plans for my future." My voice cracks. "I...I just talked to my grandpa last weekend, and he sounded so good, happy. He can't be gone." I cry.

He finishes the cigarette and again stubs it out before throwing it out the window. He pulls me to him. I wrap my arms around his neck and cry into it, again. Between the wine, the craziness of the last few days, and the crying, I'm not surprised when my eyes feel heavy and start to drift shut.

"Is she okay?" I hear, and it sounds like my mom, but my eyes are too heavy to open. The pillow I'm resting my head on is very hard, though.

I hear a man reply, "Well, uh, she cried herself to sleep, and I didn't have the heart to move her." A hand strokes my hair, and then it hits me. My professor is here, and I cried all over him earlier. "I'm Diego, by the way. I-I'm sorry for your loss." The man is always so arrogant, so it's very bizarre seeing—or I should say *hearing*—him be or sound anything less than the confident person he is.

"Thank you. Are you a friend of hers from school?" my mom asks.

"*Sí*, I am. Can we let her rest a little longer? Then I'll bring her in."

My mom's voice is soft when she answers, "Sure, thank you. Violet's been so strong for her sisters and me. It was only a matter of time before she finally let it out. Thank you again for being here for my daughter, and it was nice to meet you, Diego." She must be gone, because Diego wraps a strand of my hair around his finger.

"I know you're awake. Your mother's gone." I push myself up, and my face is inches from his. My head feels fuzzy from sleep and the wine, and all I want to do is taste his lips. Before I lose my nerve, I lean forward, touching my lips to his. He doesn't respond, and my stomach drops.

Pulling back, I whisper, "I...I'm sorry." He's not saying anything, so I go to pull completely back, but he reaches out, grabbing my face with both hands.

"*Mi espíritu libre hermoso, quiero probar sus labios,*" he whispers, and then his lips are on mine. I grab onto his forearms for purchase and sink into his kiss. Opening my mouth, I let his tongue enter. He tastes of wine and cigarettes, and it makes my breasts feel heavy, and an ache grows between my legs. My tongue touches his, and I moan into his mouth. With his mouth still on mine, he lets go of my face and grabs me around the waist, moving me until I'm straddling his lap.

My body starts rocking against his, and the friction between my legs grows into a painful ache. What's the matter with me? I've barely kissed guys, and now I'm straddling one with his tongue in my mouth. Normally just the thought of being intimate with someone causes panic to well up inside of me. Not now, though—now I want him to touch me all over.

He slows the kiss before I'm ready, but I know it's for the best. This is so wrong on so many levels. He's an asshole, for one. He's also my professor. Diego—or Professor Torres—kisses me one more time before pulling away, but he rests his forehead on my shoulder. My hands sift through his hair, and it's softer than I thought it would be. He takes a shuddering breath before lifting his head, and he grabs me around the waist. Placing me back where I was before.

Our panting breaths echo in the treehouse. I don't know what to do or say, but I'm waiting for his rejection to come. "I am sorry about what happened in class. Making you take that call was so wrong and an asshole move." He grabs my chin and tips my head back so I'm looking him in the eye. "I'm really sorry about your *abuelo.*"

Tears spill over as I stare into his dark brown pools. "I miss him already," I whisper, and now it's my turn to lay my forehead on his shoulder as I begin to cry again.

"Come on, let's get you to your family." As I continue to cry, he helps me down the ladder and with an arm around me, leads me into the house. My dad spots us first, and he comes rushing toward me.

"Daddy," I cry as I rush to him. He hugs me tight, and I bury my face in his chest.

Chapter Eight

Diego

The sound of Violet's cries and watching her collapse against her father shift something inside of me. I ache to be the man comforting her. How can I be jealous of her own father? What is wrong with me?

I can't get the taste of her off of my lips, the feel of her straddling my lap. The hairs on the back of my neck stand up when I feel eyes on me. I turn my head and find Joe, Violet's cousin, staring daggers at me. I've never been one to be easily intimidated, but this guy looks like he could pound me into the ground. He starts walking toward me, but I turn back toward where Violet's dad and now mom are hugging her tight.

"How do you know Violet?"

I turn to look at him. "School." That's all I give him and walk away. The crowd in the house has thinned out, and it seems to be mostly family.

One of Violet's aunts stops me and hands me a

plate of food. "Eat." I take the plate, thanking her. Moving through the house, I sit in one of the chairs in the living room, and as I eat, I watch the video that's playing. Violet's in a lot of the pictures, and it's clear to see that she was a beauty when she was a baby all the way through her teen years.

Watching the pictures of her family makes me long for my own back home. My parents are amazing, as is my brother. We grew up in a family that laughed, danced, and played a lot. I'm not sure why I've never been married or in a serious relationship. It's not like I didn't have the best possible role models—Hell, my brother is happily married too.

I've never had my heart broken, so there's no story there—me as the broken man who, with the love of a good woman, is healed. Like I've said before, I have always had terrible taste in women. That is until now. Violet's beautiful, smart, and ballsy, but she's my student. We'd be crossing a line that could get me fired and could get Violet kicked out of school.

A few minutes later, Violet's dad brings her into the living room and has her sit down next to me. "I'm going to get you some food," her dad says to her.

"I'm not hungry," she whispers.

"Violet, you're eating something." The words slip past my lips before I can stop them. I fully expect her to give me some snotty retort, but I'm floored when she mutters, "Fine." Her dad stares at us for a beat, and I force myself to look relaxed and like it's no big deal.

My eyes follow him as Violet's dad walks across the room and then disappears into the kitchen. Neither Violet nor I speak as we sit side by side, our thighs almost touching. I pull my handkerchief out of my suit jacket. I grab her by the chin and turn her face toward me. With gentle ministrations, I wipe the tears from her eyes.

I need to stop touching her—every time I do, all I want to do is claim her in every way possible. A throat clearing has me turning and pulling my hands away from Violet's face as her dad hands her a plate of food. Mr. Carmichael, or Dustin, again watches us as he backs away.

Around the room various family members are eyeing us suspiciously, but I don't care. I grab Violet's plate off of her lap and fork up some of the pasta salad and hold it out to her. She stares at it and at me before leaning forward and taking a bite. Bite by bite she eats the variety of foods on her plate. My dick is very fascinated by this whole situation, and it's going to get me killed. I'm a big guy, but around her family I feel like a shrimp.

She finishes the entire plate, and I feel better knowing that she's eaten, but it hasn't escaped me that her family is still watching us. "Thank you," Violet whispers.

I stretch my arm out over the back of her chair and play with her curls. "You're welcome." My eyes find her dad staring at me like he doesn't know whether to thank me or kill me. He'd want to kill me if he knew the things I wanted to do to his daughter.

It's not too much later before I take my leave. I

say my goodbyes to Violet's family and then ask her to step outside with me. Silence surrounds us as we walk side by side to my rental. "I'm staying at the Beaufort Inn. I'll be in town until Sunday if you need to talk."

"O...Okay." She gives me her phone number, and I tell her that I'll send her a text later so she'll have mine. With reluctant steps, I move toward my door and climb in. I want to tell her to get in. I want to feel her lips on mine again, I want to worship every inch of her body, and I want to know what it sounds like when she comes. What is wrong with me? I know it's wrong and what the consequences could be, but I don't care. She's dangerous, and she doesn't realize how much.

As I pull away, I watch her watch me leave from the rearview mirror until I turn the corner and she disappears from sight. I make it back to the quaint little inn and strip out of my jacket as I step inside my room. I open the bottle of bourbon that I bought earlier today and fill the tumbler halfway full and slam it down, welcoming the burn. What possessed me to come here and see her? I pour another glass and sip that one.

A knock on the door pulls me from my thoughts. I set my drink down on the desk and go open the door. "Violet?" She doesn't say anything—she just stares at me. I almost think something is wrong with her until she moves toward me with unsure steps. "Violet, don't," I whisper, but I don't believe my own words. When she's a hair's breadth away, she reaches up and cups my cheek. Violet's eyes follow her thumb as she rubs it back and forth against my skin.

How could such a simple move turn me on so much? My lips crave the feel of hers against mine again. Lord help me, I'm about to cross a line I'm not sure I'll be able to stop if I cross it. I pull on her arm until her lush body crashes into mine. She lets out the most adorable squeak before I'm kicking the door shut and attacking her lips with an urgency that can't be explained. A moan leaves her as I tease them with my tongue. I can tell she's not very experienced by the way she tentatively touches hers to mine. I can't believe I missed it earlier.

We move toward the bed, and I slowly lay her down, continuing to kiss her as my weight eases down on top of her. A groan slips past my lips because her body fits mine perfectly. Her legs wrap around my hips, and I can feel the heat coming from her pussy. I rock against her trying to ease the ache in my dick, but all it does is make it worse, especially when Violet moans into my mouth.

Her body trembles against mine—she's got to feel it too, this strong invisible pull that seems to make me lose all sense. I grab the tie at Violet's waist and gently pull until the black fabric parts and then make quick work of the tie on the inside. Pulling away reluctantly from her mouth, I look down at her bared body.

Utter perfection—she's all curves and swells and lightly tanned, smooth skin. *"Bellísima."* My voice is hoarse from arousal. My hand starts at her neck and slowly makes its way down her body, paying special attention to her beautiful breasts. The black lace bra leaves little to the imagination. Over the material, I wrap my lips around the turgid tip. Violet cries out, and her back arches, pushing more into my eager mouth. I reach out with my other hand to squeeze the flesh of her other breast. Her natural breasts are better than any fake tits I've ever had my hands on. I switch breasts and lick and suck the tip through the lacy material, but this time my free hand moves slowly down her slightly rounded stomach and down to her matching black lace panties.

Her body's trembling intensifies as my fingers slip under the tops of her panties. I pull away from her breast and look down at her. "What's wrong?"

She bites her lip and turns her head away, but I grab her chin to make her look at me. "Violet, what is it?"

"I'm scared." Her voice is so quiet I almost don't hear what she says.

"What are you afraid of, *mi espíritu libre hermoso?*"

"I...I've n-never had sex before." She shuts her eyes tight, and I don't miss the way her lower lip trembles. I should take this as my chance to stop things now. A virgin...I guess I'm not surprised since she didn't seem like an experienced kisser. The idea of being the first man to ever touch her does things to my insides and makes my cock even harder.

"Are you sure you want to do this? We can stop now and forget this ever happened. This is your call, Violet." I wait with bated breath for her answer.

"I'm not ready. I...I'm sorry." A part of me is

slightly disappointed, but the other part of me is relieved. She's a virgin and my student, plus she's bringing out this side of me that scares me. In a room full of her family, I stepped right in to take care of her and to make sure she ate. I'm just going to chalk this up to a major lapse in judgment.

I climb off of her and help her to her feet. Her hands are trembling too bad to tie her dress, so I do it for her. Once I tie her belt on the outside, she bolts out of my room before I can stop her.

I sit heavily on the end of the bed, running my hands through my hair. *What the fuck happened?* Her trembling felt like more than just fear of losing her virginity, but it's really not my business—it can't be. Thank God she had the sense to stop us from doing something we'd surely regret. I just hope that things can go back to normal.

***

Two weeks have gone by since that night Violet came to me and we almost crossed the line. On that following Monday, I wasn't sure if she was going to come back to my class or not, but I was thrilled when she was already sitting in her seat when I entered the room. I wanted to go to her, hug her, but instead I walked right to my desk and began the lesson.

I've gotten the occasional call or text from Penelope, but I ignore them. She's a pain in the ass, but at least she hasn't shown up at my home. I've gone out and have tried to pick up women, but none of them can hold a candle to *mi espíritu libre hermoso,* and I end up going home…alone.

Never have I gone this long without sex before. I've dreamt about sex more in the past two weeks than I ever have. I'm too old to be having wet dreams, but the things Violet has done to me in those dreams make my body react to the fantasy of her. It's a little disappointing that the past two Mondays she hasn't come to my office, but I should just be glad that she's still attending my class and didn't drop it like she had threatened, even though I wouldn't blame her.

I leave my office and head down the hallway to grab a quick coffee from The Drawing Board. While waiting for my order, I let my eyes drift around the room and spot Violet sitting in the corner with her nose buried in a book. Pulling out my phone, I send her a quick text.

Diego: What are you reading?

Leaning against the counter, I watch her pick up her phone, biting her lip as she reads the text. Even in the muted lighting I can see her cheeks turn the most adorable shade of pink. Violet casually turns her head until she's looking at me with those huge brown eyes. I give her a tiny chin lift, and I can't miss the way her lips tilt up in the slightest smile.

Violet looks down at her phone, and as I watch her fingers move, anticipation fills me to see what she's going to say. My phone dings, and I look down.

Violet: I'd rather not say.

Diego: Oh yeah, why's that?

She sneaks a quick glance at me before tapping away on her phone. In the meantime, the barista hands me my coffee, and I sit at a table far enough away from Violet that we can't speak to each other but close enough that I can see her, like *really* see her.

I pick up my phone and glance at it.

Violet: I'm reading a romance novel that my sister bought for me.

Diego: Romance, you say? What's it about?

I press send and set my phone down, taking a sip of the hot brew. I wait with bated breath to see what she says back. My phone dings, and I pick it up.

Violet: Well, it's about a girl who meets a mysterious stranger and he "teaches" her things.

My cock is throbbing in my pants right now just thinking about the delicious things I would love to teach her. Fuck, I want to fuck her so bad right now. I take a deep breath, trying to get myself under control before I type back my response. My eyes meet hers across the coffee shop, and it's hard to miss the way her chest expands and her breathing accelerates. I know I need to look away, to break the connection, but I don't. Instead my cock aches as she licks her lips. Doesn't she know how sexy she is? That it's a huge turn-on watching her do it? Not imagining that my cock was in between those fuckable lips?

I pick up my phone and type out a text that I know I shouldn't, but I can't help it.

Diego: I'd like to teach you lots of things.

Before I can take it back, I hit send.

Violet picks up her phone, looks at it, and then freezes. *Oh shit*, did I go too far? I drink the rest of my coffee down and plan my escape when I hear my phone *ping*. I grab it and take a deep breath before I look at it. My eyes drift toward her as I replay her words in my head.

Violet: Oh yeah, what kind of things?

Violet's bottom lip is in between her teeth. Violet's cheeks are the sweetest shade of pink as she turns toward me. I raise my brow as I keep my eyes on her, picking up my phone.

Looking away only to type out my response, I choose my words carefully.

Diego: I would rather show you than tell. Come to my office in five minutes.

I get up and make my way out of the coffee shop. My shoes echo on the linoleum as I head down the hall to my office. The whole time I ask myself what the fuck I'm doing. What if she turns me in? What if she becomes another Penelope? I should just grab my messenger bag and leave. I could text her and tell her I was just joking.

Instead I step inside my office and rub a hand over the top of my head. My brain tells me I'm stupid, but my dick wants to stand up and applaud me. I sit on the corner of my desk and stare at my door. My ears listen for the sound of her shoes on the floor, but I hear nothing. The ticking of the clock that hangs on my wall is the only sound I hear. Most of the staff is gone, so it's very quiet.

When ten minutes have passed, it hits me that she's not coming. A part of me is relieved, but a part of me is disappointed, which is ridiculous. I stand up and move around my desk to grab my laptop and shove it in my messenger bag. I turn toward the door to leave and freeze.

Chapter Nine

Violet

My stomach turns as I make my way toward Professor Torres's office. I wipe my sweaty palms on the skirt of my dress as my steps bring me closer and closer to him. I don't know what I was thinking, flirting with the man like that. Truth be told, since he showed up in Beaufort for my grandpa's funeral, I haven't been able to stop thinking about him. My mom and dad both keep asking about him, and so far I've been good at deflecting the questions. It's been a challenge to pretend to be unaffected by him.

I dream about his lips on mine and about all of the naughty things he could do to my body. The way he was always watching me made me feel hot and like my skin was too tight. I've never had this reaction to any other man before, and I'm not really sure how to handle this.

After getting his text to meet him in his office and watching him leave, I got up and went into the bathroom. I used the toilet and then washed my hands before checking myself in the mirror. Flipping my head down, I shook out my hair. When I flipped my head back up, I ran my trembling fingers through it until I was satisfied with the way it looked. I pulled my powder and lip gloss out of my bag, and with quick swipes, I applied my wine-colored gloss and then brushed my powder on.

As I make my way toward his office, I feel my heart start beating a fast rhythm in my chest. I take some deep breaths as I get closer and closer. The hallway to his office is empty, but I still walk on silent feet. I stop outside of his office and don't hear anything inside. It took me longer than five minutes to come, so maybe he's gone. When I start walking again, I reach the doorway and find him grabbing his stuff to leave.

He turns around and freezes when he sees me. Neither of us says anything as we stare at the other. Professor Torres—or Diego—is a gorgeous man with his dark hair and his dark eyes.

Diego's the first one to speak. "Come inside and shut the door." I do as he says and stop in the center of his office. He moves toward me, stopping when he's right in front of me. His hand cups my cheek. "You are so incredibly beautiful. There's this light that seems to always be shining on you. It pulls me in, and I can't seem to make myself stay away from you." His voice is low, his accent thick. I could listen to him speak all day long.

"Thank you," I whisper. God, I'm such a nerd.

"So…you want me to teach you some things?" We're practically touching. I can smell the coffee he drank earlier on him mixed with his spicy cologne. It's a heady mixture that makes my lady parts wake up and sing.

"Y...Yes?"

"Are you asking me or telling me?" His hand slides into my hair, and he tips my head back.

"Telling you." I barely get it out before his lips are on mine. Diego's lips are soft, but the kiss is hard, punishing. He wraps his free arm around me until his hand is resting on my ass and pulls me in closer. My arms find their way up and around his neck. His grip tightens in my hair, and I feel myself get wet. Should I be embarrassed that I'm so turned on already? Diego uses his lips to open mine and slides his tongue inside. Instinctively my tongue duels with his. My head swims as my body seems to light up for him.

My stomach comes into contact with his hard dick, and a tiny bit of fear hits me, but I force it back and just enjoy the feel of his lips and his tongue. A whimper escapes as he ends the kiss and pulls slightly back. "If we do this, you can't tell anyone. I know that's bad, but we don't have much of a choice. The consequences could be bad for the both of us." He takes a giant step back, rubbing his hands through his hair until it's standing on end. "Please be sure you want to do this."

Was I? Maybe he could help me get past my fear, and then I could actually consider having relationships. I could tell him why I'm still a virgin, and he could help me. He interrupts my thoughts and grabs my hand. "Come over tomorrow night. We'll talk. Nothing will happen if you don't want it to. Okay?"

Okay, I could do that. Maybe I could tell him about my mom and how that kind of messed me up, and then there was Abby's assault. Then he could decide if he really could help me or I was a lost cause, destined to be an old maid. "Okay, let's...let's do it."

He pulls me toward him one more time, but this time he kisses me slowly, sensually. As soon as I get home, I'm going to have to masturbate. My clit throbs in time with my heartbeat. *Jesus*, if I'm like this now, what'll it be like when he finally sleeps with me?

Diego pulls away. *"Te veré mañana."* In what I assume to be a sensual haze, I head out of his office and outside, taking a deep breath to calm my racing heart as I hustle home. I need to start preparing myself both mentally and physically for this.

***

I stare at myself in the mirror, critiquing my lingerie I purchased this morning at Victoria's Secret. It's a burgundy silk and lace combo. My breasts look high and perky, and the color shows off my light olive skin tone. My panties barely cover my girlie bits, but they're making my ass look great. I slip a black maxi dress down my body, loving the way it hugs my curves. Last night I'd gone and had a Brazilian wax, and fuck me, it hurt. I wanted to punch the girl doing the waxing so bad. I admit that being bare down there makes me very aware of my pussy. I've been turned on ever since.

My hair is a mass of sable brown curls on top of

my head; it's just too hot to have my hair on my neck. I grab my bag and my phone and head out to my car. This morning he had texted me his address and asked me what my favorite drink was.

The whole drive to Diego's place, I battle the nerves that have taken up residence in my belly. A short time later, I pull up in front of a lime green shotgun home. It makes sense that someone who loves architecture and teaches it would live in this style of house. I'm eager to see the inside and if it's as beautiful as I think it is. As I grab my bag and climb out, the front door opens, and he's standing there, bathed in the sunlight. A strong tingle hits me between my legs.

"Hola, mi espíritu libre hermoso." He surprises me by kissing me, outside where anyone could see us. "Come in." With a hand to the small of my back, he leads me inside. I don't try to hide my pleasure at seeing the inside of this place. The living room is gorgeous with its hardwood floors, high ceilings, and soft yellow walls. A blue and white sofa sits against the far wall with a beautiful landscape painting above it. Blue drapes hang from the windows, but they don't block any of the natural light.

A flat screen TV is mounted to the wall above the brick fireplace. Two plush sitting chairs flank the wall catty corner to the sofa. A gorgeous chandelier hangs in the middle of the ceiling, giving it an elegant vibe.

"Your place is beautiful." I don't hide the awe from my voice. He leads me into the kitchen. The walls are a light taupe color, and the cabinets and backsplash are white, and white marble countertops complete the look. He pulls out a stool at the center island, and I sit down.

"We'll finish the tour later." My eyes follow him as he grabs a bottle of wine out of the refrigerator and sets it on the counter. He pulls down two wine glasses, pouring a generous amount in each. "Here." I take the offered glass, taking a sip of the Chardonnay.

"Thank you." I look around his kitchen, wondering how much he cooks. "I love shotgun homes. There's just something about them that makes me giddy. If I owned a home here, this is the style I'd choose. Normally the color of the outside would seem obnoxious, but it just works. I love the dark teal shutters as well. I don't think it would fit if it were just some normal, boring color."

Diego grabs his wine and then comes around to sit next to me. "Did you have trouble finding the place?"

"No, thank God for GPS. I love the neighborhood. Lots of little ones around."

"Yeah there are, but thankfully they're fairly well behaved. This place was a little rundown when I bought it, but with time I got it decorated and designed just how I wanted it."

I look around, a little shocked. "You did this yourself? I'm impressed."

He picks up my hand, lacing our fingers together. "Come, I'll show you the rest." He pulls me to him so my body is flush against his. "You look beautiful, by the way." My cheeks heat up, and my nipples feel embarrassingly hard. Diego leans forward, burying his nose in my neck. Shivers wrack my body as I feel his tongue lick my skin. A moan rips from my throat as his teeth bite lightly into my sensitive flesh. "Fuck," he whispers hoarsely and then backs away from me.

Diego grabs my hand and leads me to some French doors I didn't notice before. He points out a little garden oasis in the backyard. A patio set is on the paved portion, while a fire pit sits toward the end of the yard with several chairs and a hammock. He points out a little fountain under the tree, and I ask him if he made it himself. Diego informs me that he designed it but he had someone come install it.

We move down the hall until we're in his bedroom. A king-size bed takes up a majority of the space on one side. The wall behind it is a dark gray with built-in white shelves. Black silk sheets are on the bed, which looks so comfortable I just want to climb into it. A grayish wood makes up the nightstands on both sides of the bed, with black-brushed lamps on top of them. On one nightstand, there's a docking station for his phone.

The rest of the walls are a light gray with white trim. The space is masculine and clean. The bathroom right off of the bedroom is gorgeous. A huge clawfoot tub sits in the corner with a glass shower behind it. Double sinks and two mirrors line the other wall made up of brown, natural-looking stone.

"This is what I love about these homes. From the outside they look so small, but when you step inside, it's like a whole new world. It's big and spacious."

***

Diego

My chest wants to puff up with pride as I watch Violet react to my home. It's obvious she knows her architecture, because she admires it with a talented eye. Her standing in the middle of my bedroom is doing things to me. My cock is so hard right now, and I don't want her to see it and run. I try to think of anything I can so it'll go down before she notices.

I watch her as she heads back into the bathroom, running her hand along the top of the sink. Violet crosses her arms across her chest, giving me a better view of her ample cleavage. "It truly is beautiful. The natural-looking rock in the shower looks amazing. It makes me want to take a shower in it."

She has no idea what her words are doing to me. I want to bend her over my bed and pound into her until she's screaming my name.

The timer in the kitchen goes off, and I lead her back to the stool, refilling her wine before grabbing potholders to get artichoke dip out of the oven. "Can I help with anything?" I turn to find Violet standing up.

"No, baby. You sit and enjoy your wine. I'll have everything ready in a moment." I set the dip on a plate and lay out different crackers and hard breads. Earlier I had sliced up some veggies and made some homemade dip. I set everything up in front of where Violet and I are sitting. She's poured us both some more wine and set the bottle on the counter.

"This looks amazing." I watch as she leans forward, inhaling. She turns to look at me with a sweet smile on her face.

"Help yourself." She grabs my plate first and begins filling it for me. I'm a little stunned as I watch her load it up and then set it in front of me. Only then does she fill her own plate. "Thank you," I tell her with a hand on her arm.

She's silent as we eat our appetizers. I don't know if it's nerves or what, but I don't like it. "Tell me, Violet. What scares you about men?" Violet freezes and slowly turns toward me. I reach out and tuck a strand of hair that fell out of her bun behind her ear. "If you want me to teach you, I need to know what I'm up against. Violet, whatever you tell me is between you and me. I promise that I will not share it with anyone."

Violet's hands are clasped together in her lap so hard that her knuckles look white. I reach out, covering her hands with mine. She takes a deep breath, and her eyes drift back up to mine. "When I was fourteen, we were doing this family tree project. I wanted to surprise my parents with it so I didn't tell them what I was working on. I collected information from both sets of grandparents, but I was looking for more. My dad had a safe in his home office that kept all of the important papers: social security cards, birth certificates, and medical records. I was sneaky and figured out where my dad kept the combination for it.

"One night while my parents were out and I was watching my sisters, I snuck into his office and got into the safe. I made notes of everything I found, but there was a manila envelope buried at the bottom that was dated the year I was born." Violet takes a shuddering breath. It's clear that whatever she's about to tell me is something hard for her to say. "I opened the envelope and found police reports, medical reports, and photos of my mom. Before she married my dad, she was dating a DEA agent, but then she found out he was married with kids.

"Of course she dumped him, but then he started stalking her and messing with her and my dad. One day he showed up at my mom's place. He knocked her around and then confessed that he'd poked holes in all of the condoms and was trying to get her pregnant so she couldn't leave him. After they fought, he ended up killing himself. My dad had been framed for drugs and firearms, so it was my uncles Dylan and Luke who found my mom and called the ambulance. She was in fact pregnant, but there was a chance she would miscarry due to the trauma." Violet looks at me. "Sorry I'm babbling. I started having panic attacks—I was certain that the monster who hurt my mom was really my father.

"I was afraid to know the truth, but my dad finally got the truth out of me. He was so amazing. He took me to the hospital and we got a DNA test, which proved what he knew all along and that I was his daughter. He also told me it didn't matter what the test said, but to me it did." She looks at me. "We never told my mom about it—we didn't want to bring up those bad memories."

"Wow, I'm sorry your mom went through all of that. Are you afraid that something like what your mom went through could happen to you?" I grab my wine, taking a generous sip.

"Yes, but that's not all. Three years ago, my cousin Abby was raped. Diego, it was so bad after it happened. She started using drugs and sleeping around. We all watched helplessly while she fell apart, and then six months after, she tried to commit suicide. She finally got help and is married now to a wonderful guy, pregnant with her first baby and adopted mom to a beautiful little girl. Sorry, I'm rambling on and on. Anyway, after all of that, I was just really leery about guys." She claps her hands together. "Well, that's my story in a nutshell."

Chapter Ten

Violet

Nothing like verbal diarrhea to ruin an evening, but what did he expect would happen? I stare at him, waiting for him to respond. My mouth feels dry, and I grab my wine, drinking the rest of it down. I shouldn't have done this. He's going to think I'm a freak. Blowing out a breath, I slide off the stool until I'm standing in front of Diego.

"Where are you going?" His brow is furrowed.

"I-I was going to leave." Diego reaches out and grabs me by my hips, spreading his legs so he settles me between his legs. My heart starts to beat rapidly in my chest, and a warmth pools low in my belly.

"Please don't leave. Let me throw dinner in the oven and we'll take our wine and sit outside." He reaches up, grabbing my face and pulling it down. "I need to taste you." Our lips meet in a slow glide, my arms wind around his shoulders, and I open my mouth to his seeking tongue. If having sex with this man is anything like kissing him, then I'm in for a treat. Our tongues duel, and his hand slides up into my hair, grabbing it to hold me immobile.

I should be freaking out. I should be pushing him away, but instead I feel something that I can't name, but it makes me feel warm and content. A whimper escapes me as Diego pulls away. He kisses the tip of my nose before whispering huskily, "Sit, and let me put dinner in the oven." About as graceful as a bull in a china shop, I flop down on my stool and watch Diego pull something in a pan out of the refrigerator.

After he puts it in the oven, he comes back to me. He grabs the bottle of wine and grabs our glasses and leads us out to his patio to two wrought-iron chairs with oversized, brightly colored cushions. I sit down and feel like I'm sitting on a cloud. Diego hands me my glass filled halfway, and I take a sip.

"I'm sorry that all of that stuff has happened to your family. I can certainly see where it might make you a little skittish around men. How are you and your family handling the death of your grandfather?"

My nose burns. It's only been a couple of weeks, and I still keep waiting for him to call me and make sure I'm doing my homework.

I clear my throat. "My mom and grandma are both having a tough time. Sometimes I feel like I should take the rest of the semester off to go home and make sure they're okay. I've caught myself twice reaching for my cell phone to call him and then remembering that he's gone." I quickly swipe away the tear sliding down my cheek.

"*Lo siento, mi espíritu libre hermoso.* I'm sorry, I did not wish to make you upset." He looks regretful.

"No, I know you didn't. It's just still so fresh in my mind. It's hard to believe that he's gone. Since I can remember, he and I have always been so close. Don't get me wrong, he loved my sisters just as much, but he and I had a special bond." I hear my phone ring from inside, but I ignore it.

"Go ahead and answer it. It could be your family."

Inside, I grab my phone out of my bag and see it's my mom. Her ears must've been burning. "Hey, Mom."

"Hi, baby. Are you busy?" Her voice sounds sad.

"I'm at a friend's house right now, but I'm never too busy for you. What's going on?" I close my eyes against the burning when my mom's cries carry through the phone. "Mom, where's Dad?"

"H-He took the girls over to Abby and Ben's to babysit and then was going to meet Dylan for a beer."

"Mommy, why are you crying?" I know the answer to that question. I imagine I'd be the same way if I lost my father.

"I-I miss him already. Baby, he was so proud of you. I know I've told you that a lot, but it's so true. You girls were his w-world."

"It-It's okay to miss him. We all loved him and still do. He was proud of you, too."

We only talk for a few more minutes before she lets me go. I close my eyes, and I hug my phone to my chest. I start when I feel Diego's arms wrap around me.

"Are you okay?" His voice is soft, soothing.

"Y-Yeah. I need to text my dad and tell him what's going on." He nods, and I turn back to my phone.

Violet: Dad, Mom just called. She's not doing well. She broke down.

Dad: Shit! She told me she was fine. I'm heading home now. Love you, baby girl.

Violet: Love you too, Dad. Call me if you need to.

Dad: I will.

I put my phone back in my purse. Without thinking, I walk right into Diego's arms and wrap mine around his waist, burying my face in his neck. What is wrong with me? I don't cry, but my nose burns and my throat convulses as I swallow the lump in my throat, or at least try to.

His arms wrap around me, and he gently strokes my hair. A sense of calm comes over me. Warmth spreads through my body as his closeness relaxes me. This man is like my own personal Ativan. The lump disappears, and my nose stops burning. I pull back and look into his dark chocolate eyes. My heart starts beating rapidly in my chest, and my cheeks flush.

"You feel it, don't you?" His voice is husky,

thick with something...desire? Lust?

My head bobs slowly up and down. Butterflies take flight in my belly as he pulls me close again. His hand slides into my hair, gripping it at the base of my neck. The hold is slightly painful but weirdly calming.

"Stay with me tonight." He doesn't ask—he's telling me. "Nothing is going to happen. I just want to hold you."

"I-I don't have any of my stuff," I say weakly, knowing that isn't a good reason for not staying.

"You can sleep in your bra and panties. I have an extra toothbrush, and I have face wash." One of his hands slides down my back until it reaches my ass cheek. He gives it a rub and a squeeze. "I swear that sleep is all that's going to happen."

"Okay. I'll stay." *What the hell am I doing?* is all I can ask myself over and over. Diego kisses my lips and then deposits me back on my stool before moving around the kitchen, finishing dinner. I offer to help, but he ignores my offer and gives me a smile.

"Will your mom be okay?" he asks as I watch him chop lettuce.

"I'm sure she will be. I just hate her crying, but if I'd lost my dad, I would feel the same way. Are you close to your parents?" I take a sip of my wine.

"*Sí*, we're very close, my brother too," Diego says with a soft smile on his lips. "Don't get me wrong—we were no angels, but we had a very good home life, lots of love."

I watch as he moves smoothly around his kitchen. It's apparent that he's got some kitchen skills. Conversation stalls while he finishes whatever it is that he's cooking. It smells fantastic, that's all I know.

A while later I'm following him onto the patio, where he has candles lit that I hadn't seen before. He sets our plates down and then pulls out my chair. One thing I've learned is that he's very much the gentleman. I sit down, and he bends his head, touching his lips to my cheek. This man has some mad skills of seduction. He is straight out of those romance novels my mom loves to read. I'm a horror fan myself.

I look down at my plate and inhale the delicious scent of the chicken burrito bowls, or at least they look like burrito bowls to me. I dig in and moan around the first bite. The chicken is not too salty, savory, and with a little bit of heat. "This is delicious."

"Thank you. It's my mother's recipe. It's called *Arroz con Pollo*." God, I love when he speaks Spanish.

Maybe he'll let me cook for him sometime. I could make him my grandma and mom's specialty, *Caruru de Camarao*. My grandma makes it for me every year for my birthday.

"Well it's really good. Maybe I can share my favorite dish, which is from my grandma's native Brazil." I don't miss the way his eyes light up when I mention making a meal for him.

"I knew you had a little Latin in you."

"I'm actually a quarter Brazilian. My grandma is from São Paulo. She moved to America when she was nineteen. As soon as she met my grandpa, she knew she'd never leave." I push the sadness away as thoughts of my grandpa try to enter my mind. I take a sip of my wine.

We make small talk as we both finish our dinner. When we're finished, I stand before he can stop me and take both of our plates into the kitchen, scraping them off into the trash. I can feel the heat of Diego's body as he comes up behind me. His touch is light as he places both of his hands on my hips and presses his lips against my ear. "You didn't need to do this."

"I know, but you made such a nice dinner I figured it was the least I could do." Side by side, he works with me until we have every dish washed and the food wrapped up and in the refrigerator.

He makes some coffee and tells me to go have a seat in the living room. A moment later he joins me with two cups. I can taste the vanilla in my coffee, and it smells as good as it tastes. His hand rests on my thigh. It almost seems like he's trying to get me used to his touch or at least get me to relax. Is he going to expect sex from me now?

As a matter of fact, he didn't. We watched a movie—honestly, I couldn't tell you what movie it was or who was in it. Diego's body so close to mine kept me from concentrating. A couple of times he leaned over, whispering for me to relax.

***

In Diego's bathroom, I quickly change into one of his button-up shirts after brushing my teeth, washing my face, and then using some men's moisturizer he had. I run a brush through my hair until my curls are soft and loose. Taking a deep breath, I reach for the door handle and make my way out and into his bedroom. His bedroom is empty, so I move quickly to my bag and grab my Kindle out of it. As I set my bag back down, Diego comes into the bedroom. I watch as his eyes start at my feet and travel all of the way up to my face. I'm no expert, but it's obvious that he's got an erection.

Why isn't this scaring me? Any other time I'd have been running for the hills. My anxiety would kick in, but now…nothing. Okay, well maybe I'm a little nervous. I've never slept in bed with a man before. Sure, I've slept with Joe, but we're cousins and best friends. "Do-Do you have a side of the bed that's yours?" I shift from foot to foot as I wait for his answer.

"No, *mi espíritu libre hermoso.* Climb in while I get ready, and I'll sleep on whichever side you don't." He grabs something out of his dresser drawer and then disappears into the bathroom. Diego always calls me *"mi espíritu libre hermoso"*—I need to Google it or ask him what it means. I know *hermoso* means beautiful, but beautiful what?

The mattress is like lying on a giant fluffy cloud, but it's also firm. I wiggle around until I find my sweet spot, burrowing deep into the covers. I begin reading the book that I bought the other day and immediately get lost in the story. My sisters and cousins have always teased me about loving horror books and movies. They've never bothered me. Oh sure, they scare me, but not that much. I guess I've always loved that they get my heart pounding and get me on the edge of my seat. Now don't get me wrong, in movies I am not a big fan of the gore, but it's fake and I always remind myself of that.

A few minutes pass, and Diego steps out of the bathroom. My mouth dries up immediately as I openly gawk at him. His body is lean; his skin is the color of a light caramel. His chest is slightly hairy, and he's got a little trail of hair going down his stomach and disappearing in his pajama bottoms. The large bulge in his bottoms is hard to miss. "You should probably stop staring at me like that."

His eyes twinkle as he smiles at me with a devilish grin. He climbs in next to me, and my heart begins to race. Out of the corner of my eye, I watch him turn to the side and grab something out of his nightstand. He's holding a book and an eyeglass case. Diego slips on a pair of black-rimmed glasses, and if it's even possible, he looks even hotter. Before he catches me, I turn back to my book.

I'm lost in my story when I feel his hot breath on my neck. Goose bumps break out all over my body, and my nipples become painfully hard. "What're you reading?"

"Um...I'm reading *End of Watch* by Stephen King. How about you?" I look at him, his face close to mine.

"I'm reading *The Girl on the Train*."

"Oh, I've wanted to read that. You'll have to let me know how you like it." We both settle back and are reading when I feel his breath on me again. "Yes?" This time I don't look at him.

"Why don't you read romance? Isn't that what

women like to read?"

I shut my Kindle off and turn to look at him. "I don't know. Even when I was younger, I wasn't a fan of them. Did you know I love horror movies too? Yep, I'd rather watch a good slasher flick than a romance or a romantic comedy."

"Wow, really? I would never peg you for a horror fan. Don't take this the wrong way, but you're very much a girly-girl."

I don't take offense because he's right—I *am* a girly-girl. I love makeup, doing my hair, and wearing dresses all of the time. "Oh what, because I don't dress emo? I just like them because they're exciting, they get my heart pumping, and sometimes the twists are so good that they have you shaking your head in disbelief."

"Hmm…very interesting. I like it. What's your favorite movie, then?" He puts his book down.

"Okay, this is going to seem weird, but my favorite movie is *The Silence of the Lambs*. I know it's technically not a horror movie, but it scared the crap out of me. I didn't like *Hannibal*, but I loved *Red Dragon*."

"I don't know if I've seen those. Maybe you'll have to watch them with me."

I like the sound of that. I like it so much.

Diego shuts the lamp on his side of the bed off and then leans over me to shut off the lamp on my side. His body brushes against mine, and then he settles on his side of the bed. As darkness engulfs the room, I lie stiff as a board, staring up at the ceiling. What happens now? Should we be cuddling? Should I roll over until I'm up against him?

He makes that decision for me. His arm wraps around my waist, and he pulls me toward him, my back pressed firmly to his front. One of Diego's legs slips in between mine, and he's partially covering me.

Will I be able to fall asleep like this? Of course, I don't have much time to think about it before my eyes grow heavy and drift shut.

Chapter Eleven

Diego

For the past two weeks I've tortured myself every chance I've gotten by having Violet sleep over. I've had to jerk off so many times in the past two weeks that I'm surprised I haven't worn my dick raw. I know that she's getting more comfortable around me because she immediately snuggles into me every night we sleep together with no hesitation. Her light floral scent has covered my sheets, and I hate when I have to wash her scent away.

So far we've still only kissed, and this is slowest I've ever gone in any relationship. Is this a relationship? Sure, I've cooked for her. She's cooked for me, we've snuggled on my sofa and watched movies, but I haven't taken her out. I know why I haven't. It's the fear of being caught by a student or another member of the faculty. I should stop this. I should tell her this isn't a good idea. Violet is special, and she deserves someone who can make her feel special every single day. Someone who can take her out. If I take her out, I'd be worried the whole time that someone might spot us.

I want her. I want her so bad that I ache. The ache is what's driving me to keep pursuing her when I should say forget it. This past week in class, it was extremely difficult to treat her like any other student. What pissed me off was she wouldn't even look at me—she would raise her hand and answer questions, but she looked anywhere but at me. Violet seems to be dealing with our relationship just fine, which pisses me off.

On Wednesday, one of the guys in class got a little too close to my Violet, and I wanted to knock him right out of his chair. Had I been a dog, I would've growled at the bastard. How dare he get close to my girl? I tried to tell myself that she shouldn't be mine, but I wanted her, and I wasn't going to stop until I had her...consequences be damned.

A knock on my office door has me lifting my head. *What the fuck.* "Penelope, what are you doing here?" I get up from my chair and walk around my desk, not bothering to hide my displeasure from her.

"Come on, baby. I gave you some space, but this has gone on long enough." How this grown woman thinks it's cute when she pouts like a toddler is beyond me, but since her parents spoiled her rotten, what else could I expect?

With all of my might, I try to keep my cool. She'll make a scene if I don't handle this delicately. "It's a beautiful day out...why don't we grab some coffee and go outside?" The bitch gives me a blinding smile.

As we head toward the coffee shop, she wraps her arm around mine. I try to pull away, but she practically digs her talons into my bicep.

I do a quick scan of the place and hope to God that Violet isn't here. Thankfully, she isn't. We order our drinks, and I purposely ignore her while she tries batting her eyelashes at me, blathering on about whatever it is. I hand Penelope her coffee and grab mine as I lead her out the building. We're heading down the exterior stairs when Penelope snaps.

"Watch it, you fat bitch." I see the person she ran into and freeze. Someone upstairs must hate me, because it's Violet, and she's looking up at me from where she's picking up the stuff that fell out of her bag. I go to bend down and help her, but Penelope stops me. "Don't help her—she should've watched where her fat ass was going."

Violet's eyes fill with tears. Penelope looks at me with a satisfied smile, but one look at my pissed off face and her smile dies. "Baby, don't be mad."

"Don't call me baby; we're done. I was just trying to be nice, but clearly that isn't going to work. We're done, we've been done, and the fact that you came to my place of employment just shows me I made the right decision. Stop calling me, stop showing up where I am, and just leave me alone." My voice is as quiet as a whisper, but I know I've got my point across when she drops her drink right at my feet, flips me the middle finger, and tells me that I'll be sorry.

Forgetting about her, I turn to help Violet, but she's gone. I run up the stairs and back inside, searching the entire building and coming up empty. In my office, I pull up her personal file to get her address. This is so wrong, but that's the only place I can think of that she'd be. I know she's not working at her waitressing job. She only does it on the weekends.

She lives only a couple of minutes away from campus in some nice apartment. I try calling her, but it goes directly to voicemail. The door to the inside of her complex is locked; pressing the buzzer for her unit does nothing, no answer. I move along to the parking lot and scour the cars hoping to find hers, but I don't.

I drive around some of the restaurants and coffee shops near campus and again come up empty. It's like she's vanished. Maybe she just needed to call off. I'll give her the rest of today and tomorrow—she's got my class, so she'll just have to talk to me.

***

It's ten after nine, and Violet has yet to show up to my class. I've been sitting in here for the past hour hoping to see her, but instead she's a no show. Violet has History of Architecture and Urbanism with Professor Jacobs after, and maybe if I dismiss my class right on time I might be able to hang out down there just outside his door. I'd give anything to see her, talk to her, or to have her floral scent wrap around me. My mind shifts back to teaching mode as I dive into the lesson.

Once class is finished, I hustle out of my room and head downstairs to Professor Jacobs's class. The door is shut and the lights off. I look down at my watch and see that technically the class doesn't start for another twenty minutes. It'll look a little suspicious if I just stand out here waiting for her. I head downstairs to The Drawing Board to grab a cup of coffee and hopefully run into Violet.

The coffee shop is crowded when I step inside. My eyes do a quick scan, and I spot her. She's sitting next to some asshole and their heads are together as they look down at a book. I want to go to her, but instead I watch her from across the shop. Her hair is piled up on top of her head in a haphazard bun. Her face is free of makeup, and from where I stand, it looks like she's in an oversized t-shirt…weird. Since I've known her, the only time I haven't seen her in a dress was when she spent the night with me.

If she's trying to downplay her looks, someone should tell her that it's not working. Violet's still one of the most beautiful women I've ever seen. I continue to watch them and let out a relieved breath when another girl joins them and kisses the guy sitting with Violet. The three of them talk for a little longer before they all stand up, presumably to head to the class she has next.

I step out of the coffee shop and impatiently wait for her to exit. When she does, I clear my throat. "Ms. Carmichael?" Her body goes rigid, and she turns toward me. I don't miss the hurt I see in her eyes before she masks it.

"Yes, Professor Torres." Her voice is flat, almost

robotic.

"Do you have a second to talk in my office?" I keep my tone professional and courteous, even though I want to grab her and beg her not to be upset by that stupid bitch and her jealous comments. Penelope is everything that Violet could never be: shallow, jealous, dumb, bitchy...the list could go on and on.

"No, I'm sorry. I have to get to my next class." She begins to walk away, but I stop her with a hand on her arm. I immediately let go when I realize what I've done.

I move a little bit closer to her. "Please talk to me. Let me explain. I promise you that it's not what it looked like. Yes, I used to date her but broke it off because she's not a nice person. She showed up out of the blue and wanted to talk. Her favorite thing to do is make a scene, so I just wanted her out of the building before I told her to leave." I lean in closer still. "You know the things she said were untrue, right? Baby, she's just jealous; you're so beautiful—not only on the outside, but the inside too. Cutting people down to feel better about herself is her favorite pastime. Can we talk later? Please?"

This girl makes me feel desperate. I've never had someone make me feel this way before.

"Fine," is all she says before disappearing among the other students as they head upstairs. I feel eyes on me and turn to find Clint staring at me with an odd look on his face. I give him a chin lift before heading down the hall to my office.

***

I'm just pouring myself a hot tea when there's a soft knock on my door. I wasn't sure if she was going to show or not, but I had hoped she would. When I open the door, I give her what I hope is a gentle smile and step back so she can enter. Violet doesn't say anything when she enters but follows me into the kitchen.

"Tea?" She nods her head and sits down on one of the barstools. I pour some milk and put a little bit of sugar in her cup before sliding it to her across the counter. "Thank you for coming." Grabbing my tea, I sit down next to her and grab her soft hand. "I am so sorry, baby. Believe me when I say, *mi espíritu libre hermoso,* these past two weeks with you have been the best two weeks of my life. Being with you has meant something to me, and I would never throw it away."

She answers me softly. "Okay, I believe you."

Relief fills me, and I feel myself relax. How did I think I was ever going to be able to stay away from her? The need for her is so strong that I can't imagine what it'll feel like after we've actually slept together. I reach out, stroking her cheek with my thumb. Does she realize she just leaned into my hand?

My hand moves around to palm the back of her neck. Violet licks her lips nervously just before I pull her face closer to mine. I lick softly at her lips, and as her mouth opens in a cute little gasp, my tongue thrusts into her mouth. She's becoming more confident each time we kiss. Her moan fills my mouth as our tongues duel. I let go of her neck and palm both of her full breasts. My thumb grazes her nipples, which harden immediately.

I want to shout in victory as her arms make their way around my shoulders and she begins to pull me close. My hands make their way under her t-shirt and again cup her breasts, which are covered in the softest cotton. This is about as far as we've gotten. I'm on my way to sainthood due to the restraint I've had to show. She's saint and sinner wrapped in the sweetest package I could ask for.

Letting go of her breasts, I grab her thighs and pull her legs up until they're wrapped around my hips. With no self-control, I grind my hardened dick against her pussy.

She shudders almost violently against me, and my cock tries to punch its way through my pants. The cutest whimper leaves her lips as I start rubbing against her pussy in a slow, sensual pace. Her tongue rubs against mine and vibrates with each moan that leaves her lips.

My dick is so hard right now. It's aching to get inside her tight pussy. Every natural instinct is demanding that I pull down her pants and rip her panties away. It's demanding that I unleash my dick and push it inside her virgin pussy. Instead I pull away, her lips chasing mine and pouting. I groan as I release her legs and see the wet spot on the crotch of her gray leggings. Now I want to taste her, to see if she tastes as sweet as I imagine.

It does something primal to me as I look at her face and take in her lust-filled eyes. Her lips are swollen, and she has pink cheeks. "Fuck, I want you so bad right now." My words come out as a growl. Violet surprises me by grabbing my face and pulling it down to hers. She attacks my mouth with a hunger that matches my own. It's a gnashing of lips and teeth, and I can't control myself. My hand slides inside her leggings and into her panties.

My fingers slide through her wetness, and she moans against my mouth as I gently rub her clit and then move down to her opening. Fuck, I have to taste her. I pull my fingers out of her panties and pull my mouth away from hers. Holding her gaze, I bring my fingers up to my lips and suck the wet digits into my mouth. Her taste explodes on my tongue, and I want to drop to my knees thanking the Lord for this.

"You taste as good as I thought you would." My lips descend on hers. Can she taste herself? Does she like it? My home phone rings, pulling us out of the moment. I groan when the answering machine kicks on—yes, I still have a home phone and an answering machine. My mom's voice comes over the line.

"*Mijo,* you need to call me. I haven't heard from you in a week, and you know I worry. Don't make me call again. I love you." I turn back to Violet, and she's giving me a sweet smile.

"You're in trouble," she says in a singsong voice.

"Oh no, *mi espíritu libre hermoso,* I think *you're* in trouble now." I grab her sides, tickling her until she begins to squeal. She struggles against me until she finally slides off the stool and takes off running. "You can't run from me, baby." I sprint through my house, finding her hiding in the darkened corner of my bathroom. She screams as I grab her, throwing her over my shoulder and then down on my bed.

I straddle her body and pin her arms down. She smiles up at me as her chest rises and falls. "Now that I have you, what am I going to do with you?"

I bend down to kiss her neck. I love the sound of the sigh that leaves her lips, but the sound of her stomach growling has me pulling back and chuckling. "Is my girl hungry?" She nods her head. "Okay, let's get you fed." I reluctantly climb off of her and then help her off of the bed.

Chapter Twelve

Violet

My bedroom looks like my closet exploded all over it. Tonight Diego is taking me on our first official date. It's been a week since his ex-bitch ran into me outside of the building at school and called me fat. Things have been amazing between Diego and me, but I can't seem to give him my virginity. No matter what I've done, he's the one who always pulls away. I obviously know he's attracted to me. There was never any mistaking the erection in his pants whenever things get heated between us. He must have some amazing restraint, because I've been ready to pounce on him all week. What is it about the man?

Wednesday after class, I hung around for a few extra minutes, wanting to perfect the design I was working on when I felt him come up behind me in the empty classroom. His fingers touched me so lightly I thought for a second that I had imagined it. When he pulled up a chair to sit next to me and look at my design, he did it with his hand on my bare thigh. Over the past week he's had me so close to orgasm that when he touched me I almost exploded right then and there.

He didn't do anything more than touch me, but it was enough. Diego gave me constructive criticism that he gave the others too, not just me. He helped me see my strengths and weakness with the project and all without giving me the upper hand on my classmates, which I appreciated. That was one thing that we both agreed on—that I wouldn't get treated any differently.

I didn't want to be treated differently, and now I'm freaking out. I settle on a dress that's the color of Merlot, a deep rich burgundy. It hits me right above my knees and has a gauzy overlay that has brown and burgundy swirls all over it, and it definitely keeps with the free-spirited look that I love. I put on a pair of wedge espadrilles that wind around my ankles and are tied in cute bows.

Bangles are on my wrists, and I'm wearing chandelier earrings that match. My hair hangs down in loose waves, and my eyes are smoky. I put a little bit of gloss on my lips. In the bathroom, I stare at myself. *Ugh, he's going to think I look fat*, I think but try to push the negative thoughts away. What if he doesn't show up? What if he thinks I'm boring? My mind starts to conjure up every negative outcome possible. I close my eyes and take some calming breaths.

There's a knock on my door, and I know that it's got to be Diego. One more time I glance at the mirror as my hands tremble slightly. I inhale and exhale slowly, reminding myself that he's made it clear that he thinks I'm beautiful. Making my way toward the door, I unlock it and pull it open. The man oozes sex; he's wearing a fitted black dress shirt tucked into a pair of gray slacks that don't hide his bulge.

He's holding a bouquet of lilies. "These are for you, and can I just say that you look so fucking beautiful." I step back so he can come in, and when he walks by, his musky scent fills my senses. As soon as I shut the door, his arms are around me and his lips are on mine. My hands grab his sides and hold on as he assaults my mouth. With a moan, I open my mouth to allow his tongue inside. Our kiss is cut short when he pulls back. "You make me lose control." His lips are a hair's breadth away from mine. "Every time I pull away from you, my body screams at me, telling me I'm making a mistake."

I take the flowers from Diego and walk them into the kitchen. Under the sink, I grab the vase that my sister, Daisy, made for me and set it on the counter.

Diego picks it up. "This is beautiful. Where did you buy it?"

"My sister made it, actually. Daisy is very artistic."

I watch him turn it all around, admiring it while I trim the ends of the stems. After he fills the vase with water, I place the flowers in it and then set it on the table. I excuse myself and grab my overnight bag out of my bedroom and place a shaky hand to my stomach before heading back out into the living room. Diego's looking at some family photos I have hanging on the wall.

"You and your mom and sister all look alike. Daisy looks like your dad, doesn't she?"

I smile as I look at the picture. "When we were little, people used to think Lilah and I were twins, and now that we're older, people think that our mom is our sister. Daisy is Dad's mini." Diego grabs my overnight bag and then my hand. After I grab my purse, we make our way out to his car. Being quite the gentleman, he opens my door for me and then shuts it when I'm inside.

The soft, supple leather feels nice against my legs as I put my seatbelt on, watching Diego walk around the front. He places my bag in the backseat before climbing in the driver's side. "I like your car." God, I'm stupid. What a dopey thing to say.

He grabs my hand and kisses my palm. "Thanks, baby."

We make our way toward Bourbon Street to a little jazz/dinner club. It's seven in the evening, and there is already a line out the door, but Diego tells me he made a reservation. Once we park, he wraps his arm around my waist as we head toward the front of the line. The hostess looks up as we approach, and it's not hard to see that she's salivating over my man. She comes out from behind her podium in a tiny, and I mean tiny, little black dress.

My body tenses as she gets close, but I realize that she's got menus in her hands and is taking us to our table. I roll my eyes as I watch her shake her ass as she leads us to a table in the darkened corner. He pulls out my chair for me, and I sit down. Before he can seat himself, the hostess places her hand on

Diego's arm and actually purrs when she tells him to enjoy his meal. All he does is nod his head and then sit down next to me.

I love the fact that the place is illuminated by candles everywhere, and it gives the room, with its dark wood floors, red walls, and black tables, a romantic feel. A soft, passionate beat fills the room. Our waiter comes, we order drinks, and Diego orders us an appetizer.

"Tell me about Spain. Where are you from? What's it like?"

He drapes his arm on the back of my chair and fiddles with my hair. "I'm from a town called Náquera. It's not small, but it's not big either. It's gorgeous. We're nestled in a valley surrounded by pine trees."

"Does your family still live there?" Our waiter brings our drinks and our appetizer. Diego asks him to give us a bit before getting our dinner order.

"Yes, my mom and dad do. My brother and his family live in Valencia. It's huge compared to Náquera. It's nice, though—it's only about a half hour away, so it's easy for my parents to see their grandkids. Plus he still commutes to our hometown for work."

As we eat our appetizer, he tells me about his family, and I can tell how much he loves them. Especially his nieces and nephews—he can't stop smiling as he talks about them. It's nice to know that he's close to his family too.

A little bit later, the waiter comes and takes our order, and I order another drink. While we wait, I feel his hand on my bare thigh. He spreads my legs a bit under the table and begins to stroke the inside of my thigh with his thumb. Goose bumps pop up all over my body, and I begin to tingle between my legs. "Is this okay?" His lips are against mine.

"Yes," I breathe out. "I-I like when you touch me."

He kisses my lips, slowly and surely. In between kisses, he whispers, "Good. I plan on touching you a lot. The feel of your soft, silky skin is enough to get me turned on."

Our waiter interrupts us to take our order, and surprisingly Diego doesn't move his hand from my thigh as he orders his food and then mine. The waiter disappears, and Diego leans forward. "Tonight, nothing will happen unless you want it to." He cups my cheek with his palm. "If all you want to do is snuggle, then that is all we'll do. I'll even take you home if that's what you want."

How can this man banish any sort of anxiety I feel when I'm not close to any other member of the opposite sex who isn't family? I grab him by the front of his shirt and pull him toward me. His eyes widen in surprise before my lips are on his. It's a soft kiss, a kiss that lets him know what his words meant to me.

Our food arrives, and conversation stalls while we both eat. Every few bites, Diego forks up some of his duck and offers it to me—it's hot and a little sweet and absolutely delicious. I feed him some of my Creole pork chop. We both finish our meals, and then the waiter clears our plates away. The live musicians are setting up on the stage, and Diego excuses himself to use the restroom. The man exudes so much confidence that when he passes by others, they take notice.

While he's gone, I check my face in my little compact. I apply a little more lip gloss and pop a mint into my mouth. He comes back a few minutes later, draping his arm across the back of my chair and toying with the ends of my hair.

***

Diego

For the past hour, I've watched my girl be spun around the dance floor by older men, and when I say older, I mean old enough to be her great-grandfather. She smiles and laughs as they move her around the dance floor. Men and women alike watch her with rapt attention. Her joy is palpable and—enough, is *enough*. *I* want to dance with my girl.

I make my way toward the dance floor. She sees me coming and whispers something to the man that's dancing with her. Like a gentleman, the old-timer leads her to me and then kisses her cheek.

I pull Violet into my arms, and we start moving to the music. She fits perfectly against my body, like she was made for me. Her body moves with mine like we've been dancing together forever. She's shared with me that she's danced since she could walk, and by the way she moves it's obvious that she's good at it. There's this light that shines in her eyes that is filled with so much joy I can't help but feel the same.

Violet looks around and then turns back to me. Her smile fades. "Aren't you worried that someone will see us together?"

I'm taken aback by her question. "You know—I didn't give it much thought today." That actually scares me, but I won't tell her that. She's a distraction to my sanity, but I feel like I could fall for this girl and fall hard. "Don't worry. If something happens I'll take care of it."

Violet's lips turn up in a small smile, and she whispers, "Okay."

We dance for a little while longer before taking our leave. Her arm is around my waist as we make our way down the street to my car. On the road back to my place, sexual tension fills the inside of my car. I swear if I take a deep breath that I'll be able to smell her arousal. She's clenching her thighs together and biting her lip. I reach out and rest my hand on her thigh, stroking the soft skin.

When we reach my place, I turn to look at her. "Baby, look at me." She does. "Whatever happens is all up to you." I wrap my hand around the back of her neck and pull her toward me, placing a soft kiss on her lips. Reluctantly, I pull away and tell her to wait while I grab her bag out of the back and come around to help her out.

My hand's on the small of her back as we head up the walkway to my front door. I unlock and open it so she can step inside ahead of me. My cock is hard as hell as I watch the sway of her hips as she walks into my kitchen. I lock the front door before following after her. She's pouring herself a glass of water. From behind, I wrap my arms around

Violet's waist. I brush her hair out of the way and kiss her neck, smiling when I feel her body shudder against mine.

I pull her hips back until her ass is against my dick. My hands slide up the front of her dress until I'm cupping her breasts, feeling her nipples harden against my palms. "*Mi espíritu libre hermoso.* You were made for me. Did you know that?" My tongue makes a path up her neck to her earlobe. I nip at it and smile as she moans. Massaging her tits and grinding my cock against her ass causes a groan to rip from my throat. "Your body fits perfectly against mine."

With quick movements, I spin her around and attack her mouth. She immediately opens her mouth to me, my tongue entering her mouth in sinuous strokes. Her hand slides down the front of me until she's palming my cock. She gives it a squeeze, and my knees practically buckle. With all of my might, I pull back and watch Violet's eyes slowly open, and she stares up at me.

"I want you to stay here for a minute. I'll come get you when I'm ready."

She smiles. "Okay, I'll wait." I make my way into my bedroom and pull the bin out of my closet.

Chapter Thirteen

Violet

I take some deep breaths as I wait for Diego to come out and get me. My whole body is one giant tingle right now. I'm embarrassingly wet too. Nervousness and excitement fill me as I wait. Soon my virginity will be gone and I'll know that I can handle being close to a man because let's face it, sooner or later Diego will get rid of me. There are just too many obstacles in our way, and soon enough he'll realize that he could do better than me. *Now is not the time to freak out,* I think.

My heart starts to race when I hear his bedroom door open and the soft padding sound of his feet on the hardwood floor. Warmth spreads through me when he appears in the doorway. His shirt is untucked and unbuttoned, showing off his black undershirt, and his feet are bare.

"Come here, baby." His voice is so seductive, and as if I'm in a trance, I move toward him. Diego holds his hand out to me, and I slide mine into his.

He leads me into his room, and my mouth hangs open. Every available space is filled with lit candles, giving his bedroom a soft, romantic look. Soft music plays in the background. "What do you think?" His breath tickles my ear.

"You didn't have to do all of this, but I love it." My smile is wide as I step farther into the room.

"Of course I did. Your virginity is something special, and I want it to be an experience that you remember." I wrap my arms around Diego's waist and hug him tight. He kisses me tenderly before whispering, "Turn around, baby." I do what he says and give him my back. Slowly, he slides down the zipper, the noise echoing in the room.

My dress slides down my body and pools at my feet. Diego moves until he's standing in front of me. I want to cover myself, and he must be able to read my mind because he slowly shakes his head. "Don't hide your body from me." He looks me up and down. "Pure beauty." Thank God for Victoria's Secret. I'm wearing a matching Champagne-colored satin bra and panty set. He helps me step out of my dress. "Now take my shirts off."

With shaky hands, I reach out and stick my hands under the shoulders of his button-up shirt and push it off of his shoulders and down his arms until it floats to the floor. I grab his muscle shirt from the hem and pull it up and over his body, dropping it to the floor as well.

"Get on the bed." His voice is low and authoritative, and I immediately do as he asks. I watch as he climbs onto the bed after me, coming up between my legs until his face is inches from mine. Wrapping my legs around his waist, I pull his face down to mine and kiss him. Our kiss goes on for a while before he begins kissing down my neck, nipping at the sensitive flesh.

It's not long before he's traveling down again until he reaches my breasts. He reaches behind me and unhooks my bra, then tosses it on the floor next to the bed. Diego grabs both of my breasts and then his tongue descends, swirling around one nipple while he pinches and pulls at the other.

Heaviness grows between my legs, and moans leave my lips as he suckles at my breast. He switches breasts, and I cry out as he nips at my turgid tip. I grind against the bulge in his pants, hitting my clit and pushing me closer and closer to orgasm. Diego's hands slide down my sides until he reaches my panties. There's a tugging and then the unmistakable ripping sound and then they're gone.

It hits me that I'm completely naked, but I don't even have a chance to worry about that because he begins kissing down my body. Goose bumps break out all over my body as his tongue drags across my stomach and then down to my hipbones. We've only done oral sex one other time, and it had been weird at first. Then when I finally relaxed it had felt amazing.

He spreads my thighs wide seconds before his tongue swipes at my damp folds. My hands go to his hair as he opens me wide, fucking me with his tongue. I should be embarrassed by how wet I am, but right at the moment I can't drum up enough energy to worry about it. My moans and cries echo in the room as he continues to lick, suck, and repeat over and over again. He swirls a finger around my opening and begins working it inside of me.

"*Dios, eres tan apretada.* You're so tight, baby. My cock is going to love being buried deep inside of you." My womb clenches as he works his finger in and out of me. The noise my body is making because I'm so wet should embarrass me, but it doesn't, especially since Diego keeps groaning and growling against me. He sucks my clit between his lips, sucking hard as he finger fucks me.

Pressure builds, and when Diego reaches a certain spot inside of me, I explode. Waves and waves of pleasure fill me, my back arches off of the mattress, and my eyes feel heavy. I open them to find Diego standing at the end of the bed stripping out of his pants and boxer briefs. My throat dries as I take in his beautiful body. He's muscled but lean. My eyes follow the strip of hair that runs from his belly button down to his large dick. Now granted, I don't have much experience, but it's the prettiest cock I've ever seen.

Licking my lips, I watch as Diego climbs back on the bed, coming toward me like a predator stalking his prey. His mouth reaches mine, and I can taste myself on his lips. It's tangy and different but not necessarily bad. My hands slide up into his hair as my tongue tickles the seam of his mouth. My legs wrap around his waist as his tongue begins to duel with mine. The kiss goes on for a while before he pulls back. "Are you ready for me?"

I nod, but that's not good enough. He wants to hear me say it. "Yes, I'm ready." He pushes away from me and reaches into his nightstand, coming back with a condom. With his teeth, he opens the packet and then pulls the latex out.

I watch him as he quickly sheaths himself and then lines himself up with my pussy. "We're going to go nice and slow, baby." He pushes in ever so slowly until just the head is inside me and he hits my hymen. After that, he begins to work himself inside me inch by inch. I feel like I'm going to be split in two. In and out he works me over while he kisses me slowly, taking my mind off the inevitable pain.

He pulls almost all of the way out before thrusting back inside me until he's buried to the hilt. I cry out against his mouth, and a tear leaks from my eye as the pinching, burning feeling hits me. He holds himself deep inside me and begins to kiss me all over my face. Diego brushes my hair out of my face and looks at me with a tender look that melts my heart.

The pain fades, and I need him to move. I begin wiggling under him, and he takes the hint. He pulls almost all of the way out before easing back into me. This time a moan rips from my lips. Pressure builds down below, and I tingle as he moves in and out, in and out. He bends down, pulling my nipple into his mouth, sucking it with strong pulls that have a direct line to my clit, which is pulsing so hard right now. He grabs my thigh, lifting it higher up his body, sinking even farther inside me, if that's even possible. "You feel as good as I thought you would. So wet, so tight, and so hot."

"Oh God," I moan. He lets go of my thigh and reaches in between us and starts rubbing my clit. I spread my legs so he sinks inside me a little bit more. The rubbing gets faster and he moves in and out, in and out until he slams into me and my body detonates. My nails score his back, my neck arches, and his mouth finds my neck, biting and sucking the sensitive skin. When my unintelligible cries begin to slow, he picks up his pace, slamming into me over and over until he buries himself deep and I can feel him throbbing inside of me.

I close my eyes and let my fingers trail up and down his back. My ankles lock around his lower back, and my arms wrap around his shoulders, hugging him tightly. "That. Was. Amazing." My lips are near his ear.

He rolls us so I'm on top, straddling him. His dick is still inside me, making me so full I squirm, and he rolls us again so he's on top, but this time his softening cock slides out of me. Diego places a kiss on my lips before climbing out of bed. "Give me two minutes and then come join me."

I watch his gorgeous naked ass as he walks away from me, and I want to squeal right now. Why didn't I believe my cousin Carrington when she told me that sex was amazing? Sure, I still have a lot to learn, but that was so good. Diego made me feel so special, and no matter what, I'll never forget this.

Once I feel like I've waited long enough, I step tentatively into the bathroom to find Diego filling the bathtub. He smiles when he sees me and sticks out his hand, beckoning me to him. "You're going to be sore. This will help with that." With my hand in his, he leads me toward the tub.

"Are you getting in with me?"

"Do you want me to?" I nod and then gingerly step into the tub. Diego follows behind me. He sits down first, and then I sit in between his legs. My back rests against his front as he lies back, taking me with him. At first we're both silent, both of us just enjoying the warm water as it laps over our skin. His strong hands massage my shoulders, relaxing me to the point I feel my eyes drift shut.

"Baby?" A voice pulls me out of my sleep. "Violet?" My eyes flutter open, and I realize I'm still in Diego's bathtub.

"Oh my gosh, I fell asleep. I'm sorry." I turn my head to look up at him. He tilts my chin up and kisses me softly on the lips. My stomach chooses that moment to growl, and loudly.

"Come on, let's get out and I'll make you a snack." Diego gets out first, wrapping a towel around his waist. He comes back to the tub with a big fluffy towel for me. After helping me stand, he gently dries me off and then wraps the towel around my body. In his bedroom, I grab my nightgown out of my bag and slip it on over my head. Diego throws on a pair of basketball shorts that sit low on his hips, making my mouth water even though I am a little sore between my legs.

"No, baby. Don't look at me like that. You're going to need a little time to recover before we do it again."

***

The sunlight shines in through the skylight, waking me slowly. Diego's warm body is practically on top of mine, almost like I'm in a safe cocoon. The ache between my legs isn't as bad as I thought it would be…thankfully. Last night after our bath, I sat at the counter while he made us a couple of sandwiches. We munched on those while watching a movie, and then I fell asleep, only waking as he gently stood me up and walked me to his bedroom.

I roll over the best I can and take in Diego's sleeping form. He's a lot less intimidating while he's sleeping. His facial hair is dark this morning, and it makes a rasping sound as my fingers rub against his cheek. I watch his eyes flutter open, and his lips tip up into a soft smile. "Morning, baby." His voice is roughened with sleep, his accent thicker.

"Morning." He pulls me close, kissing my lips. Apparently he's not bothered by morning breath. "I have to be at the café in two hours," I say with a pout.

"Okay, but first breakfast."

We climb out of bed, and he leaves me to shower and get ready while he makes breakfast. After I climb out of the shower, I find a cup of coffee just the way I like it sitting on the counter, and I can't help the smile that graces my lips. He's very thoughtful, definitely not like the man I met at the start of the semester. I hum to myself while I braid my hair and then put on my makeup. Back in Diego's bedroom, my uniform, which is black dress pants and white dress shirt, is lying on his bed along with my bra and panties.

I quickly don my uniform and slip on my black

ballet flats before stuffing all of my clothes into my bag and then throwing it over my shoulder. Out in the kitchen, I find Diego stirring something at the stove. He turns to me, smiling. "Come here, beautiful."

Setting my bag down, I go to him and melt as he wraps an arm around me, pulling me close to him. I tip my head back, accepting his kiss. He grabs my braid, and using it to hold me immobile, he deepens the kiss. His tongue demands entrance into my mouth, so I open to him. He finally pulls away, and I can't help but laugh because he kept stirring what looks like grits while he kissed me. "I love grits."

"Get us some coffee and I'll finish breakfast." We make light chitchat while he whips up some eggs and makes some toast. He sets my plate and bowl in front of me and kisses me on top of the head before grabbing his own. Side by side, we sit and dig into our food.

A half hour later and Diego has pulled up in front of my apartment building. He turns toward me in his seat. "I want to kiss you right now, but we're too close to campus."

I hate that we'll have to hide our relationship. Of course, that's if that is what this is. For all I know, he just wanted to bag a virgin—No, that's not it. He doesn't seem to be the type who would set out to hurt someone purposely. But still, maybe this isn't going to work.

Surprisingly, I want it to work. He's funny, romantic, kind, and he's big on pampering, which is sweet. I've always admired the relationship my parents have.

My dad has treated my mom like a queen for as long as I can remember. Hell, he's treated all of us girls like queens, and he's had four women looking after him too. Will it be worth it to pursue this even if it's a secret?

He reaches out, cupping my cheek with his palm. Can he see the internal battle I'm having? "I want this and to see where this goes. It kills me that we have to hide it, but maybe it won't have to be forever. Just please don't give up yet." His pleading tone matches the look in his eyes.

"Okay, let's see what happens." I open the door, and he stays me with a hand on my arm.

"Can I see you tonight?"

It warms me that he wants to see me again. "I really need to work on my studies." I climb out of the car and give him a wave before running inside my building to put my bag away and then grab my apron off of the counter and head out to my car.

Pulling into the parking lot of Organically Yours, I see my co-worker/new friend, Dani, getting out of her car. She gives me a wave and waits for me to get out of my car.

"Hey, Violet! How was your weekend?" I love her bubbly personality—it's genuine and refreshing.

"It was good, quiet. How about you?"

"The same. Except I worked both Friday and Saturday." She pulls open the backdoor, and I follow her inside.

***

After a long afternoon, I'm thankful to be home.

I'm so tired, and I still have some homework to do. I make a pot of coffee, and while it's brewing, I change into some boxer shorts and a t-shirt. In the bathroom, I shake out my hair and twist it up on top of my head. I pour myself a cup of coffee, set it down on the kitchen table, and pull my books and laptop out of my bag, sitting down and getting to work.

I've been studying for the past two hours and have drunk half a pot of coffee. I get up in desperate need of a good stretch. I feel a twinge down below, so I grab some ibuprofen and pop a couple into my mouth. I almost don't want the pain to go away. I like the reminder of last night.

It still boggles my mind that that man—that incredibly sexy, experienced, dominant man— wants me. That I'm not anxious when he touches me, like any other man who isn't family.

Instead when I'm around him, I feel a sense of calm and a rightness that scares me. I'm just barely twenty-two and he's thirty-four. He's also got lots of experience where I have none. I saw his ex and she was gorgeous: tall, thin, fake boobs, and platinum blonde hair. She's the epitome of what every guy wants, and my guess is that every other girl he's been with looked just like that mean bitch.

In my bathroom I stare at myself in the mirror. I know I'm somewhat attractive, but I've got more pronounced curves, hips, big boobs, and a big ass. With a sigh, I make my way back into the kitchen to make myself some dinner, and by make, I mean grab the box out of the freezer and throw it in the microwave. Oh, I can cook, but when it's just me it's sometimes too much of a bother.

I'm pulling out my chicken spring rolls when my phone rings. "Hey, Daddy."

"How's my girl doing?"

I set my food down at the table and grab a glass of water. "I'm great. School is going great too. How is Mom?" I haven't talked to her since she had her little breakdown.

"She's doing better. She's missing you and can't wait until Thanksgiving break when you come home. I miss you too, sweet girl. While I've got you on the phone, I wanted to ask you a question. The man that was here for your grandpa's funeral...that was the professor that's been giving you problems, isn't it? You keep refusing to answer every time we ask you about him."

I'd wondered when he was going to ask me again about Diego. A sigh leaves my lips, and I answer him. "Yeah, that's him."

My dad's sigh comes through the phone, and he catches me off guard. "Violet, you're not sleeping with him, are you?"

What the hell do I say? I've always told my dad everything. If I tell him the truth, he'll be here tomorrow ready to kick Diego's ass, but I've never lied to my dad. My stomach turns, and before I can think better of it, I blurt out my answer. "No, Daddy, I'm not. Why would you think that?"

"I don't know...it's just the way he watched you at your grandma's. He fed you, for Christ's sake. Promise me you aren't doing anything with that man."

"Dad, I promise. I'm not. He just felt bad making

me take your call in front of the class. That's all. He was probably sucking up to keep me from turning him in or something." I hate myself right now. I don't lie to my dad...ever.

"Okay, but you tell me if he tries anything. I'm serious, I didn't like the way he watched you."

Closing my eyes tightly, I rub my forehead. "He won't try anything, I promise. I think you were just seeing things. Now let me talk to Mom. I love you."

"I love you too, baby girl. Your mom just came in. I'll talk to you soon."

"Well hi, my baby girl! What are you doing?" My mom sounds better, which makes me smile.

"Hi, Momma. I just got done studying and making myself some dinner." I take a bite of my spring roll. "How have you been doing? I've been worried."

My mom is quiet for a minute, and I want to kick myself for saying anything. "I'm doing better, baby. I miss your grandpa every day and it hurts, but each day gets a little bit easier. Grandma is staying with us for now. She just doesn't want to be in their home without him."

"Does she want to sell it?" That thought makes my stomach hurt. I know it's selfish, but I have so many great memories of their place. Hell, the treehouse I built with Grandpa and Dad is there. It would be so wrong if another family moved in there.

"She hasn't said, but I'm thinking that she will. I can hear it in your voice that it upsets you. It's just too big for her all by herself, and without Grandpa, she doesn't really want to keep that reminder."

"No, I get it. Honestly, Mom, I do. It'll be good for her to stay with you guys. Is she in my room?"

"Yeah, I'd get her for you, but she's actually at the studio with your Grandma Carmichael and Daisy. She's showing some of her blown glass this next week. They're helping her get her pieces set up. It makes your grandma feel useful and keeps her mind busy. Your Grandma Carmichael has been spending a lot of time with her too." My dad's mom is a beautiful woman inside and out—of course she'd be there for Grandma Hutchins.

We talk for just a few more minutes, and then she lets me go so I can study some more before bed. I have two tests coming up, and one of them is in Diego's class. When we're alone, I never bring up school; I don't want him thinking that I'm with him or want to be with him for good grades. So far he hasn't treated me any differently than before. I honestly love our verbal sparring in class. He likes to keep me off balance. He pushes me and challenges me to give a hundred and ten percent.

I finish getting ready for bed a short time later and am just getting settled under the covers when my phone beeps.

Diego: I miss you.

Why does that give me a thrill?

Violet: I miss you too. What are you doing?

Diego: Lying in bed thinking about you. I can still smell you on my sheets. I love it.

If anyone could see me right now, they'd see me smiling like a loon.

Diego: *Did you have a good day at work?*

Violet: *I did. I got some studying done tonight and talked to my parents.*

We don't talk too much longer because I start nodding off, but I know I'll see him tomorrow.

Chapter Fourteen

Diego

I don't like the way the boys in my class stare at Violet, and if they don't stop I'm going to do something that I'll regret. She has no clue either. How someone so beautiful could be so oblivious to male attention, I don't know.

Right now, they're doing computer work, so I walk slowly around the room looking over their shoulders to see what they're working on. It's just a simple AutoCAD design. When I pass by Violet, her flowery scent fills my senses, and I have to concentrate very hard on not getting an erection.

After class, I grit my teeth as I watch Clint wait for Violet, and then they disappear out into the hall. I sit at my desk tapping my pen on the wood, over and over. My irritation is rising, so I make my way downstairs to grab a coffee, hoping that it keeps my temper from rising. I've had "issues" with my temper before, but that was when I was a hotheaded, hormonal teenager.

At the bottom of the stairs, I scan the area and feel my blood boil. There is a line coming out of The Drawing Board and Violet is standing in it, but Clint is standing next to her. That's not all—the shit has his hand on her. My girl doesn't seem to like it because she keeps stepping back from him.

Without thinking, I make my way toward them. "Ms. Carmichael, I believe you're supposed to be in my office for a meeting right now." I keep my scowl firmly in place. For a second she looks confused, but then she plays along.

"Sorry. I was just hoping to grab a drink before my next class." Violet turns to Clint. "I'll see you later."

She follows me silently down the hall. I feel eyes on me, and when I look behind me I find Clint standing at the mouth of the hallway staring after us. I don't like the look on his face, but I just turn back around and lead her to my office. Katherine isn't at her desk, for which I'm glad.

As soon as we clear the door, I shut it behind us and then push her against it. My lips press against hers, and it's a gnashing of lips and teeth. My hand finds its way under her dress and cups her pussy. I can feel the heat coming from it, and all I want to do is bend her over, rip her panties away, and pound into her until she's covered in my scent so no one will question whom she belongs to. I reluctantly pull away from her mouth but kiss up her neck until I reach her ear.

"I don't like the way he touches you. I don't like the way he watches you. Promise me you'll stay away from him."

"Wh-What? He's just my friend, Diego," she whispers.

I start rubbing her pussy with the palm of my hand, and she moans softly. "You just don't see it, *mi espíritu libre hermoso,* but I do. Who is touching you right now?"

"You." Her moan is music to my ears.

"Yes, me. This pussy is mine, and you're mine. No one gets to touch what's mine...ever."

Violet's pupils dilate, and I feel the crotch of her panties get wet. I press hard against her clit and rub until she moans and I have to cover her mouth with my hand. Her panties are soaked as she rides my hand, her breath hot against my palm. She shudders against me, and I'm ready to come in my pants. As she melts against the wall, I pull my hand away from her mouth. Her eyelids are heavy, and her face is flushed. "I should let you go get your coffee before your next class. Come over for dinner tonight?"

She nods her head slowly and then whispers, "Okay."

I pull her to me, kissing her lips one more time before letting her go. Once she collects herself, my gaze follows her down the hall until she disappears around the corner. "I'm so fucked," I mutter. Violet has quickly become an addiction, and every time I'm around her, it gets worse. Looking down at my watch, I make my way upstairs to my next class.

***

I'm just putting the steaks on the grill when I

hear my doorbell. I move through my home and open the door to find my beautiful girl standing on the other side. "Come in." I step back so she can step inside. I wait until the door is shut before I pull her to me and kiss her quickly on the lips. "I hope you like steak and sweet potatoes."

"Yummy. That sounds great, but I'm going to have to start running again." She makes the most adorable face, scrunching it up like she hates the idea.

With her hand in mine, I laugh and lead her into the kitchen and pour her a glass of wine. "Not a fan of running, I take it?" She takes the wine and sips.

"Not at all. I could dance at the studio for hours, but if you see me running, it's probably because someone or something is chasing me. How was the rest of your day?" I wrap my arm around Violet's waist and lead her out to my little patio.

"It was good. I had a meeting about the curriculum for next year. We're thinking about changing things up just a little bit. We're only in the brainstorming phase now."

She sits in her chair and crosses her legs, giving me a glimpse of her pink panties. I hadn't realized when she got here just how short her dress is.

"That sounds exciting. I brought my homework to work on, if that's okay? It's not that I did it for help—I just wanted to see you, but I really need to study. Is that fine?" She's babbling and won't look at me.

"Baby, go get your bag. Study after dinner. I can find something to do while you study. What class is it?"

"It's the business class that my dad wanted me to take. Every summer I work for him and my uncles, and they have me doing everything. The hands-on stuff, the plans, and the front office—he wants me to know every inch of the business."

I quickly flip the steaks. "Your father is a very smart man. Especially if you want to go into your family's business." I grab her hand and pull her up. "Go get your bag." She kisses me quick before disappearing into my house. She returns a few minutes later and sits back down in her chair.

"What made you want to teach?"

Grabbing my wine, I sit down next to her. "While I was in school, I tutored other students and really loved it. It became my passion. I know I'm tough, but I'm a perfectionist, and that is what I expect from my students." I grab her hand and bring it to my lips, kissing the back of her hand. "I know I've told you before, but you have a natural talent."

Her cheeks turn a deep shade of pink. "T-Thanks."

I get up and pull the steaks off the grill, and Violet follows me inside. She asks me what she can do to help, so I have her grab the plates and silverware. I pull the cubed sweet potatoes out of the oven and am pleased with how they have turned out. Side by side, we work together to plate our food, and then I carry our plates to the bar and set them down.

I wait for her to dig into her food, and when she moans around her first bite of the steak, I start eating. "This is amazing," she tells me in between bites.

After dinner, I tell her to go study while I clean up. When that's all done, I peek in on her and find that she's focused on her books and laptop, so I take the opportunity to go sit on the patio with my laptop and Facetime with my brother.

When Jorge's face pops up on the screen, we immediately start talking. Growing up, people always assumed we were twins because we look so much alike. He just has a little more salt and pepper in his hair.

"How are you, little brother?" I can hear their youngest squealing in the background.

"I'm well. Why is Sofia still up?"

He shakes his head. "She's got bronchitis and is on steroids, so the monster is hyper as hell. At least she's feeling better. So is that troll giving you any more trouble?"

"Not after the last time she came to the school." I tell him about her running into Violet, without really telling him who Violet is to me.

"Diego, I seriously don't know where you find these women. You need to find someone like my Marisol."

I'd love to tell him that I have. Jorge's wife is incredibly beautiful, but she's got the biggest heart and the kindest soul, making her beautiful inside and out. A lot like my Violet. Hell, even our mama is the same way. I'll never understand why I picked the wrong women until now, but in a way it's still wrong because she's my student.

"Uh-Diego, who is that?" I turn around and see Violet in the kitchen getting a glass of water. She looks up and gives me a smile and a wave.

I wave back and then turn back to Jorge. "I need to tell you something, and you really need to keep this between us. I mean, don't say anything to anyone, at least not yet, and especially Mama. That's Violet...my girlfriend." Wow, that is the first time I officially referred to her as my girlfriend, but it feels damn good to say out loud and I love it.

"Why is this just between us? Please tell me she's not married."

Really, I should be offended that he just said that, but I used to not care about any of those details. "No, she's not married. She's one of my students."

At first Jorge's silent, and then he begins to lay into me. "What the fuck, Diego? Are you stupid or what? Is this pussy really worth throwing your career away for?"

"Now listen here—she's not just some pussy. She's different, man. She reminds me of Marisol and Mama." I hear the door open, and she comes out onto the patio, but she freezes.

"Oh my gosh. I'm sorry. I'll-I'll just go back inside." She starts to back away, but I hold out my hand.

"Come here, baby." She takes my hand, and I lead her around until she's sitting on my lap. "Violet, this is my brother Jorge. Jorge, *this* is Violet."

"H-Hi Jorge. How a-are you?" I can feel her trembling in my lap, so I stroke the smooth skin of her thigh.

"*Hola*, Violet. I'm well, thank you."

Violet lifts her hand and gives a tiny wave, and I

don't know why until I realize my niece Sofia is behind her dad, smiling. Jorge looks behind him, grabs the little sweetheart, and sets her on his lap.

"*Hola, mi sobrina hermosa.*" She cuddles into her daddy and then covers her mouth as she starts coughing. "*Chica pobre bebé.*" I look back at my brother. "Her cough sounds awful."

"The sad part is it actually sounds better than it did. Marisol and I have taken turns staying home with her, and Mama has come to help too. I should probably get her to bed. I'll talk to you later." He looks at Violet. "It was nice meeting you."

"You too, Jorge. I hope she feels better. *Adiós.*" She gives another wave to Sofia and gets up. "I'll leave you alone to say goodbye." I watch her head back into the house and then turn back to my brother.

"Okay, maybe she's different from the other women, but just be careful. Is she Spanish, Mexican?"

"Her mom is half Brazilian." We sign off a short time later, and I head into the house to find her with headphones in and her nose buried in her book. I don't want to disturb her, so I grab my book I've been reading out of my bedroom and sit down next to her on the sofa. It isn't lost on me how she immediately leans into me, but my girl keeps on studying so I get lost in my book.

***

Violet sits astride me, my cock buried deep inside her incredibly tight pussy. I love that she's trusted me enough to let me teach her ways that she can get the most pleasure. Her hips swivel, causing my eyes to roll back in my head. She's a quick study, that's for sure. I grab her beautiful tits and suck one nipple into my mouth, moaning around the tip as I feel her pussy tightening. This girl really tests my restraint and my endurance. I could come right now. "Put your hands behind your head." My voice is low, gruff.

She slowly lifts her arms and then puts her hands behind her head. I let go of her breasts and lie down as I grab her hips and show her how to move. Up, down and up, down she moves. Her moans echo through my bedroom. Once she picks up the rhythm, I let go of her hips and with one hand grab and pinch at her nipple while using the thumb of my other hand to rub her clit.

She's so wet I can feel it on my thighs, and that just makes me even harder. That familiar tingle starts at the base of my spine as I pick up my speed, rubbing her clit. Her channel starts to tighten around me. Her moans have turned to cries, and she's started moving erratically on top of me. "Are you going to come for me?"

"Yes..." she moans.

I pinch her clit and thrust my hips up as she cries out, squeezing me over and over as she comes and comes hard. With a quickness I flip us over, spread her legs wide, and begin to ruthlessly pound into her. A part of me knows I should be gentle—she was a virgin not that long ago—but that primal part of me doesn't care, and I just begin to thrust into her over and over. I grab her hands and pull them up over her head, keeping them there as that tingle at the base of my spine intensifies.

My head comes down, and I suck a nipple into my mouth as my balls draw up tight. I plant myself, once, twice, and then groan as my orgasm hits me hard. I hold myself so deep inside her as I empty myself into the condom. When I let go of Violet's hands, she wraps them around me, stroking my back slowly. I know I should move—I don't want to squish her, but she locks her long legs around me, holding on tight.

I kiss her behind her ear and love when she sighs and melts against me. When I finally pull out, she whimpers.

"Let me go take care of this." In my bathroom, I dispose of the condom and wash my hands. Back in the bedroom, I find Violet getting dressed. "What are you doing? Are you leaving?"

She freezes and looks at me. "I didn't know if you wanted me to stay or not. So I thought I'd get dressed."

Still naked, I move to stand in front of her. "Don't go. Stay." She nods her head, and then she lets me take her clothes back off. I follow her onto the bed, and we settle under the covers. After shutting the lights off, I reach across the bed and pull her body until it's draped over mine. I've never been a snuggler—my side is my side, but I can't seem to get her close enough.

Her arm winds around my waist, and her lips touch my chest. "Thank you for tonight," she whispers against my chest.

"No need to thank me, baby." She kisses me one

more time before her body completely relaxes and I know she's out.

All I know is that I want to spend more and more time with her. I don't want to hide it, but there's just no way to have an open relationship with her without jeopardizing my career and her education. It would devastate me if I ruined her chance at the education she deserves. With that thought, I fall asleep.

Chapter Fifteen

Violet

"Can I get you anything else?" I ask the table of women. One of them looks familiar, but I can't place her. She's wearing a gorgeous skinny scarf around her neck, and her long thin legs are encased in boots that come up to just below her knees. It's the second week in November and it's about seventy degrees during the day, so I've been seeing more and more scarves and boots. She's gorgeous and put together, but I can just tell she's not a nice person. I don't know what it is, but there's just something about her.

I hand them their check, and they wave me away. They had me run my ass off, and I doubt I'll get a tip. Dani's pouring glasses of water when I step in the back. "What's wrong? You look mad."

Blowing my bangs back, I shake my head. "That table of women have had me running my ass off, and I'm sure they're going to stiff me. Sure, they can afford expensive handbags, but they can't tip

147

someone they feel is beneath them."

"Girls like that are just jealous when they're around competition. Violet, you're hot. You've got this whole free spirit vibe going on. You do notice that guys mostly sit in your section, don't you?"

I honestly have no clue what she's talking about.

"Okay, whatever. Have you looked in the mirror? You're a babe." I give her a wink before walking by and then jumping when she snaps me with a towel. "Bitch." I laugh. I'm so glad that I've met Dani. I've always had a hard time making friends, especially with other women. I mean my best friend is a guy, I like to build things and people assume that I'm a tomboy, but I'm totally a girly-girl.

When I make my way back out front, I see that the table of women is gone. I go to clear the table and see that they left me two dollar bills, a quarter, three pennies, and some lint. I grab it and shove it in my pocket. I'm not even mad because I knew this was coming. Oh well, karma will eventually catch up with them.

At the counter, I turn and find the blonde standing there looking at me. "You're the girl who has got a thing for Diego, aren't you?"

Oh God, that's how I know her. Penelope. "I don't know what you're talking about," I lie and start to walk away from her.

She hisses. "Stay away from him, you fat bitch." I just shake my head and head through the doors to the kitchen.

After our shift, Dani and I walk down the street to a little hole in the wall bar, which according to

Dani, has the best sausage and shrimp jambalaya. We step inside and grab a booth in the corner. Our waitress takes our order and then brings us our drinks a few minutes later.

"Where do you come from?" I ask her.

"I'm from a little town just outside of Nashville called Kingston Springs. What about you?"

I take a sip of my beer. "I'm from Beaufort, South Carolina. The majority of my family lives there and in Atlanta." Our food comes, and we make small talk while we eat. In front of me is the biggest slice of cornbread I've ever seen. The butter has a sweet taste that complements the spiciness of the jambalaya. There is no way I'm going to be able to eat this all. I'll get a to-go box and take it home with me. Maybe I'll take it to Diego.

Dani's an only child and her parents are older. She broke up with her high school sweetheart last year after he started getting rough with her. Her dad's a retired Master Sergeant from the Marine Corps, so he only had to "talk" to Dani's ex once and he never bothered her again.

I pull out my phone and show her pictures of my family and a couple of Joe and me at our graduation from high school. "Geez Violet, are all the people in your family gorgeous? Your cousin's hot."

That is the reaction I get all of the time when people see my cousin. He looks like a younger version of our dads. He's been using his looks to get the girls since grade school. I honestly can't wait to see what happens if he ever meets the one. She'll be someone who is going to knock him on his arrogant ass.

"He's good looking, but he knows it. He's a total ho."

We finish eating, and we head back to our cars. We make plans to meet for lunch in the cafeteria one day this week, and I'm actually looking forward to it. She surprises me by giving me a hug before she climbs in her car and takes off. I climb into my car and send Diego a quick text asking if he wants my leftovers and does he want me to bring it over.

He answers me almost immediately.

Diego: No thank you. Not tonight.

I stare at my phone, and I'm not sure how to handle it. This is where it sucks that I haven't really had a relationship before.

Violet: Okay, sorry to have bothered you.

After pressing send, I toss my phone into my purse and make my way toward home.

***

Coffee cup in hand, I make my way up to Diego's classroom. I don't know what's going on with him, and I'm over it. On Monday when I had walked into his class early, I told him good morning, and he merely nodded his head. At first I had been frozen like a stupid fool, but Clint coming in and looking at me oddly had me snapping out of my frozen state.

The rest of that class he didn't speak to me or

acknowledge that I was even there. After class I had taken my time leaving, hoping that he'd give me something, but instead he walked out with some of the other students. I skipped the rest of my classes that day. First I got mad, and then I shut off my feelings for him.

Now as I reach the classroom door, I'm stopped in the hall when Clint calls my name. He gives me a smile. "Hey, Violet, were you sick Monday? You weren't in the rest of our classes."

"Yeah, I didn't feel that great so I went home and laid down."

Ugh, why does he always touch me? I've tried to let him down gently, but he doesn't seem to get the hint. He rubs his hand up and down my arm. "If you want, I'll give you my notes to copy. If you want, I can study with you too."

I really could use the help, but would I be opening a can of worms that could make things awkward? "Okay, yeah that'd be great. I have lunch plans with a friend today, but maybe we could meet after my shift in the library this afternoon."

"How about I stop by and you can let me know when and where to meet?"

A throat clearing behind us has me stiffening my spine. I know it's him—I can smell his unique scent—but I refuse to look at the bastard. Who takes someone's virginity and then turns into an asshole? I thought that was something only teenage boys do, but apparently I was wrong.

"This isn't social hour, and class is about to start." He walks by us and heads inside the classroom. Clint looks at me with a raised brow. All

I can do is shrug my shoulders and then follow him into class.

Later, I move through the quad toward the cafeteria. Up ahead I spot Dani with her e-reader in her hand. She obviously has no clue I'm walking toward her, because she hasn't even looked up from whatever she's reading. "Earth to Dani," I say in a singsong voice. She looks up and sticks her tongue out at me before jumping up and sticking her device in her bag. Looping her arm through mine, we head inside.

We sit down outside at an empty table with our trays of food. "Can I get your advice about something?"

She looks up and nods. "Of course. What's going on?"

I have to be careful how I say this, because I can't let on whom I'm talking about, and plus it's over, so what does it really matter? "Well, I sort of got involved with this guy, and we slept together twice. I thought things were great, but all of a sudden I'm getting the cold shoulder. I don't know if I should confront him about it or just ignore it and move on. He's the first guy I've ever dated, and I don't know how all of this is supposed to work."

She reaches across the table and grabs my hand. "Was he your first, first?" I nod and look down at my food, which suddenly looks extremely unappealing. "Okay. Honestly I don't really have a lot of experience either, and thanks to my ex, I really haven't dated anyone either." She leans in and says quietly, "Is it Professor Torres?"

The water I just sipped comes flying out of my

mouth as I choke and cough. What the hell, how does she know? *Play it cool, Violet.* "Why would you ask that?"

"I don't know. After that day we saw him at the café and the way he was looking at you."

I don't even know what to say or do. So I do the only thing I can think of. "Um…I've got to go." I jump up and race-walk out of the cafeteria. This sucks so bad, and I've got no one to talk to about it.

"Vi, wait!" Dani is out of breath as she catches up to me outside the library. "Hey, I didn't mean to put you on the spot or anything. If you can't talk about it, I can respect that, but if you need to talk, I won't tell anyone. I promise. You're the first friend I've really made since I came here."

Can I trust her? Lord knows I can't talk to Joe about it, because he'd tell my dad for sure or fly down here and try to kick Diego's ass. "Can you come over tonight?" She says yes and she's bringing the ice cream. I tell her I've got the wine and give her my address.

Inside the library, I get to work, praying that it's not a mistake telling Dani everything tonight.

I'm pushing a cart full of books toward the back when I hear footsteps come up behind me. I turn toward it and scream when I find Clint directly behind me, totally in my personal space.

"Sorry, Violet. I thought you heard me call your name. I told you I was coming to make plans to study. Are you free tonight?"

"No, a friend is coming over tonight. Would tomorrow work?"

"Sure, that sounds good. Do you want to come

over to my place?" Clint looks at me expectantly.

There is no way I'm going to his place. "How about we meet at The Drawing Board? If we sit in the corner, the noise isn't as bad."

He looks disappointed, and I know I'm in trouble with this guy. I think it's safe to say that I can't and won't be alone with him. There is just something that is giving me the heebie jeebies. "Yeah sure, how about we meet at ten?" I agree and then feel myself relax as he walks away, but not before he turns around and gives me a weird smile and a wave.

What have I done? I ask myself as I wave back. After tomorrow, I'll see how it goes and then see if I need to I'll let him down gently.

***

The sound of the buzzer pulls me out of my thoughts. I feel like I'm on edge a bit. Opening up to someone I don't know has always been difficult for me. I press the button to let her in and open the door, standing in the doorway. Dani smiles and holds up a bag, which I assume holds ice cream.

"Hey, girl. I didn't know what kind you like so I got a variety: cookies and cream, mint chocolate chip, and strawberry cheesecake." She looks around the inside of my apartment. "I love your place. It's so cute. My parents want me staying in the dorms until my senior year. I don't know why, but it was one thing I gave my dad after the disaster with the dickhead. I think he feels I'm safer in the dorms, but at least I have my own room."

"Yeah, I understand that. My dad said in order for me to get my own apartment he had to help me find the place. He was really paranoid, but a few years ago, one of my older cousins was attacked and our safety became my dad and uncle's main concern. I can't blame him." I point to the sofa. "Have a seat; I'll put the ice cream in the freezer and grab us the wine."

I set the bottle of Moscato on the coffee table after pouring us both a glass. Dani takes her glass and then turns toward me on the sofa.

"Sit and start talking. I know we don't know each other well...yet, but you can trust me. I would never betray your confidence." The conviction in her voice makes me believe her.

"Up until a few days ago, I was dating Professor Torres. We've had sex, and I was a virgin before him." It's like I have a bad case of verbal diarrhea. "I'm sorry. I just threw it all out there."

Dani's silent at first, and I'm really starting to feel like maybe I shouldn't have said anything. "I think this requires ice cream and lots of it." She pops up and dashes into my kitchen, and I hear her rattling around in there. A minute later, she reappears with all three pints and two spoons.

I grab the cookies and cream and peel the lid off. Shoving a huge spoonful into my mouth, I moan around the creamy goodness as it melts on my tongue. "This is so good."

Dani nods her head. "Yep, it's the perfect thing for man troubles. So tell me everything. Obviously I don't expect you to go into full details, but you can give me a summary. Heck, you can tell me everything if you want. No pressure."

I end up telling her the Cliffs Notes version of everything. She doesn't respond—she just listens as she eats the mint chocolate chip ice cream. After I finish speaking, I take a huge bite of my cookies and cream. "Well?"

"Okay, I'm no expert, but after everything you've told me, all I can think of is something spooked him. Things are great between you—hell, you slept with him for a while before actually *sleeping* with him. It sounds like he's been sweet and attentive, and then all of a sudden it changes. Someone developing feelings for someone doesn't have them shut off just like that." She reaches out and grabs my hand. "If he is who you want, then you're going to have to make him tell you what's going on and why the sudden deep freeze. Violet, I promise, and I meant what I said. I won't say anything to anyone, and anytime you need to talk to someone, you can come to me."

Surprising myself, I lean forward and pull Dani into a hug. "You don't know how much that means to me. It's not like I can really talk to anyone in my family about this, and I really haven't made a lot of friends."

"Well, now you have me."

We drink our wine and eat our ice cream and binge watch *The Office*. We're both a little buzzed, so I make up the sofa and tell her she's spending the night and promise her that I'll make sure she's up for class. I have none tomorrow—I'll just be studying with Clint, which makes my skin crawl, and I don't know why.

On my bed, I stare up at ceiling. Dani's right. I need to ask him why the sudden turnaround. Why does it scare me? Maybe it's actually hearing his rejection that's scaring me. Can I do it? Can I be brave enough to ask him? I guess we'll just have to see.

***

"Lunch tomorrow? You can tell me what happened with Clint and if you talked to Mr. Professor Man."

I hug her tight. "Lunch sounds great, and I'll tell you all about both things…hopefully. Thanks for listening to me last night and for not judging me."

She pulls back and gives me a smile. "You're welcome, and I could never judge you. Maybe one day I'll share my story." Dani gives me a wave before stepping out of my apartment. There is definitely a story there. Her eyes looked so sad when she said it. I can only hope that she trusts me enough to tell me and to let me be there for her like she was for me.

I swallow down a couple of ibuprofen and quickly shower. Not wanting Clint to get the wrong idea about us meeting, I keep my makeup light and pile my hair on top of my head. I slip on a long, cotton, royal blue and black maxi dress and flip-flops. I don't have to meet him for a half hour so I quickly call my sister Lilah.

"Hey, Vi. What's up, girl?"

"Not much. Just checking in to see how everyone is doing. How's beauty school?" My sister is absolutely amazing at doing hair and makeup. She's the one that taught me.

"It's amazing. I've learned lots of tricks. I taught Abby a couple of different ways to style Natalie's super curly hair." Ben, Natalie's dad, is half-black, and she inherited his curly locks. "Daisy lets me practice on her most of the time."

"How are Mom and Grandma?"

"They're okay. Grandma is quiet a lot. She stays in her room most of the time. Mom's trying to pretend like she's okay, but just looking at her, you can tell she's not herself. I know Dad won't say anything to you, but maybe you should come home to visit. Could you take a long weekend? Maybe surprise them? They'd love it, that's for sure."

"I'll see if I can make it happen. I have to go, though. I'm meeting a classmate to study. We'll talk later. I love you, Lah."

"I love you too, Vi. Call me if you're able to come home." We hang up, and I grab my messenger bag, stuff my laptop in it, and head toward campus.

I reach Richardson Hall and find Clint standing at the bottom of the steps. He gives me a huge smile as I walk up to him.

"Hey, Clint. How are you?"

"I'm great, Violet. You look beautiful as always." Crap, I should've worn sweats.

We walk side by side into the building and make our way into The Drawing Board. I set my bag on the chair and tell Clint I'm going to grab a cup of coffee. As I stand in line, my mind starts to wander. I think about my phone call with my sister and know I need to try and come home, and soon.

Maybe if I talk to my professors, they'll give me my homework and lesson plan so I can at least work on my homework while I'm gone.

My body immediately locks up when that familiar scent starts to surround me. I refuse to turn around—I'm not ready to face him, and it's not like I can ask him what I really want to know right here anyway. I order my latte and move to the end of the counter. It's not lost on me that girls behind the counter are flirting shamelessly with Diego. I can't hear what he's saying to them, but it's probably a lie just like the lies he told to me. Ugh, my vision turns cloudy because of the tears I've refused to let fall up until now. Blinking them back quickly, I refuse to give him the satisfaction of knowing that he hurt me.

Again when he moves to the end of the counter, I can smell him and feel his body heat. Luckily the girl hands me my drink, and without looking at him, I head to the table where Clint is sitting. "Clint, did you want coffee? Sorry, I should've offered to grab yours while I was up there."

"That's okay. I had some coffee on my way here this morning, so I'm good." He starts moving his chair close to mine. "Shall we get started?"

I nod, because honestly, the sooner we start the sooner I can finish and go see if they need any help in the library for a bit.

We finish up a little over an hour later, and I'm so glad to be done. Clint touched me every chance he got. First it was his foot rubbing against mine. Then it was a hand on my arm and back. The coffee shop had filled up, so I didn't want to make a scene and embarrass him. The worst was when he draped his arm on the back of my chair and leaned in to me. His coffee breath was in my face, and I had to fight to keep my expression neutral.

I stuff my laptop and books into my bag and stand up. "Thanks for your help today. You took some great notes."

He looks at my mouth, and I take that as a cue to leave and fast. "O-Okay. Maybe we can do this again? Next time we could do it over dinner." His look is hopeful. Time to let him down gently.

"We can study again, but that's all it is. I'm sorry, Clint. I'm just not looking for anything more right now. My main focus is my family back home and school. Please understand and respect that." My heart is racing. I've never been so bold and spoken my mind like that before. I want to vomit so bad right now.

He looks crestfallen, and I start to feel bad, but I'm not interested. "Oh, okay, yeah. Not a problem."

I take my leave, but before I step out of the coffee shop, I find Clint staring at me with a strange look on his face. Shaking off the heebie jeebies, I head to the library.

Chapter Sixteen

Diego

It takes everything in me to not march over to Violet's table, grab that asshole, and throw him across the room. Clint is all over Violet, and it's making me physically ill to watch it. Why the kid can't read her signals is beyond me. She couldn't be more obvious that she's uncomfortable; her body is completely stiff, and every time he leans in, she slowly leans back.

I watch from across the shop as she stands up to leave. Violet exchanges some words with Clint, and I wish I knew what they were saying. Finally, she walks away, and I turn to look at Clint, who is watching Violet with a look on his face that gives me an uneasy feeling.

Shaking it off, I grab my coffee and head to my office and go over notes before our monthly department meeting. I know I've been treating Violet like shit, but Sunday night I found Penelope sitting outside of my home. She wanted to know who the girl was that I had spent the night with. It was a kick to the gut to know either she was watching me or had someone watching me. I couldn't risk Violet being spotted with me. It would kill me if she got caught in my mess.

I'll explain, and it'll work out for us—it has to.

I'm collecting the handouts for the meeting when there's a knock on my door. Professor Daniels is standing in the opening. We've worked together since I came to Tulane. "Hey, Mike. How are you?"

"Good. Just came to see if you were ready to head to the meeting."

I stand up and move toward the door. "How's that lovely wife of yours?" The conference room is at the end of the hall.

"Cher's great. She's hoping for some grandkids soon. Especially now that both kids are married— she's been harping on Mara since she's got a good job, and she and her husband just bought a house. Are you still dating that blonde?" One night when Penelope and I were out, we ran into Mike and his wife. Of course, Penelope acted like Penelope and completely embarrassed me.

"God, no. I got rid of her, although she's like a bad penny and keeps coming back. I don't know what I was thinking getting involved with her."

Mike laughs. "Please, it was because she was gorgeous."

"Maybe, but that only gets you so far when you've got no personality and aren't very bright."

We grab our chairs, and I start the meeting. "As you all know, the university is holding the annual charity masquerade ball at the end of January. Our department is in charge of the silent auction. If we all contact local businesses for items to be auctioned off, we should have plenty. Remember, it's black tie, so dust off the tuxedos."

To be honest, I like wearing my tux—it just gives me this sense of power. I know it sounds crazy, but it's true. Now the only thing running through my mind is me in my tux and Violet in a wine-colored evening gown.

Great, now my dick's hard. I get myself under control, and we make plans to meet in a couple of weeks to further discuss plans. When I head outside, I spot her out of the corner of my eye. Violet is walking along the path that leads toward her apartment building. Before I can stop myself, I move swiftly toward my car. I pass her up so I park on her street, climb out of my car, and sit on her steps. A few minutes later, I see my girl walking down her street and then up the walkway to me. She's almost on me when she realizes I'm right in front of her.

"Diego?" Her voice is breathy, but then she disguises it and looks at me with indifference.

"Can we talk?" She won't look at me. "Baby, please."

"Don't call me baby. You've got five minutes, and then you have to leave." I follow her inside, trying desperately not to stare at her ass. We reach her door, and I take her keys out of her hand and unlock it. With a huff, she stomps past me into her apartment. I hold back the chuckle that wants to escape and want nothing more than to pin her to the wall and fuck the shit out of her.

I stand in the middle of her living room, rubbing a hand through my hair. Violet comes toward me but stops far enough from me that I won't be able to reach out and grab her. "Well?" She looks at me expectantly.

"Sunday night, Penelope came to see me. She wanted to know who the girl was who had spent the night. Do you know what that means?" Violet shakes her head. "Either she's watching me or she's got someone else doing it. I made a split-second decision to avoid you, hoping that she wouldn't figure out that something was going on with us. She'd make your life hell, and that's the last thing that I want for you."

"Then why are you here? Why couldn't you tell me what was going on instead of making me think I made a mistake giving you my virginity?" Her voice cracks, and I can't help myself. Ignoring her protests, I wrap my arms around her and hold her tightly to my chest. She's stiff as a board.

"*Lo siento, mi amor.* I'm sorry. I promise you that you didn't make a mistake giving me something so precious." She looks up at me with her big brown eyes. "God, you're breathtaking, my beautiful free spirit, *mi espíritu libre hermoso.*" I reach up and start pulling the pins out of her hair until it starts to tumble down in silky, sable-colored curls.

My fingers sift through her soft hair until I grab it at the base of her skull. Her pupils dilate, and her breath leaves her in a gasp. I lean forward until our lips are almost touching. Her breath hits me in minty puffs. Her hands move until they're against my chest, and for a second, I'm afraid she's going to push me away, but instead she grips my shirt, ripping it open.

The ping of my buttons hitting the wall echoes through the apartment. That one simple movement causes something to awaken inside of me. A growl rips from my lips, and I tighten my grip in her hair. "You're going to do everything I say and everything I ask for, aren't you?" She blinks up at me with heavy eyelids. "Answer me."

"Y-Yes, Professor." I don't think she knows what she just said, but I won't lie—hearing her call me that while she's turned on is a rush, and if possible, my cock is even harder than before.

I step back. "Go into your bedroom, strip out of that dress until you're down to your bra and panties, and I want you kneeling in the middle of your bed waiting for me. Am I clear?"

She nods and whispers, "Yes."

"Yes what, Violet?"

"Yes, Professor." I watch as she silently walks down her hall into her bedroom.

I adjust my dick in my pants and swear he's trying to bust free. With quick movements I pull off my dress shirt, tie, and then undershirt, tossing them on her sofa. While in the living room, I toe off my shoes and then take off my socks. On silent feet, I slowly make my way toward her bedroom. My dick is throbbing with need. I've never needed to be inside of someone as badly as I need to be in her.

Just before I reach her doorway, I take a deep breath. Once I can see inside the room, I freeze in place. In the middle of her bed, looking like a wet dream come true, Violet is doing exactly what I asked. She's in a matching dove gray bra and panty set. Her curves and smooth, tanned skin are on display for me. "You look good enough to eat."

Her cheeks turn the most beautiful shade of pink. I don't miss the way she eyes my body and licks her lips. My cock pulses in my pants, trying desperately to get out. I climb onto her bed and move until we're face to face. "There are so many things that I want to do to this delicious body of yours." The image of her tied to my bed flashes through my mind.

I reach out and stroke her cheek. "Do you forgive me for being a stupid idiot?"

"I forgive you, but please tell me if something is going on. I know I'm a lot younger than you and completely inexperienced, but I don't like being kept in the dark. It's not fair to play with my emotions like that." My eyes squeeze shut as shame fills me. She's right—I didn't think about her feelings. Yes, I was trying to protect her, but I hurt her anyway.

I feel her hand on my cheek and open my eyes. She leans into me, touching her lips to mine. I sink into the kiss but then reluctantly pull away. Her eyes drift down to my dick, and her teeth sink into her lower lip. "Do you want to suck my cock, baby?"

She keeps staring at it but nods her head. I've jerked off plenty of times imagining her plump lips wrapped around my length. I get off the bed and whisper huskily, "Come here, baby." Violet crawls to the end of the bed and then climbs off. She moves to stand right in front of me. I grab her hands and help her down on her knees. God, she's a vision, and I have to close my eyes to get myself under control before I come all over myself.

She reaches up and unbuttons my pants. The slide of my zipper sounds extremely loud. Violet fishes my cock out of my pants and then looks back up at me. I grab it under the head and squeeze, trying to dull the ache and the desire to come. Her hand reaches out and wraps around my length. I cover her hand with mine and show her how hard to squeeze me and then guide her hand up and down.

"Lick the tip, baby." I watch her tongue come out of her mouth and moan as it drags across my swollen purple head. I had been worried that it would turn her off that I'm uncircumcised, but she's never even brought it up. Violet wraps her mouth around the head and slowly starts to suck. "Fuck, you're a natural, baby. Yes…just like that." I moan as she takes me further into her mouth.

I remove my hand from hers, and she begins to suck with vigor. Her head bobs up and down, and my fingers comb through her hair, holding her in place as I start to thrust into her mouth. "Harder, baby." She increases her suction, and I start thrusting faster. I'm going to come soon if I don't stop her. A part of me wants to come in her mouth, but another part of me wants to come deep inside her—fuck, the idea of taking her bare makes me want to come even more.

Her hands grab onto my hips as that familiar tingle starts at the base of my spine. I try to pull away, but she starts sucking harder. "Baby, I'm going to come in your mouth if you don't stop." She completely ignores me and keeps going. A moan tears from my lips as I begin to come and come hard. "Oh fuck, baby!" Her moan vibrates around my dick, and I feel her swallow me down.

When it finally stops, Violet slowly eases her mouth off of me. She reaches the tip and lets her tongue glide over the sensitive head.

***

Violet

I lick my lips and can taste the salty, musky flavor of Diego. To be honest, I didn't know for sure if I wanted to try giving him a blowjob, but then I couldn't think of anything else. My lips had been stretched tight around his length, and when he grabbed my hair and started fucking my mouth, I almost lost it. I felt dominated by him, and it turned me on even more.

Diego reaches down and strokes my cheek with his fingertips. Warmth spreads through me, and I move to stand up, but before I can, his hands are under my arms and I'm flying through the air. I hit my mattress with a small bounce and a giggle, which quickly turns into a moan as he first rips my bra and panties off of me then grabs my thighs, spreads them, and buries his tongue in my pussy.

My hips fly off of the bed, and his hands move until they're pinning my hips down. I grab handfuls of his hair as my body gets closer and closer to orgasm. He blindly reaches up and grabs both of my breasts, pinching the nipples enough to give me a bite of pain. Diego sucks my clit into his mouth, sucking hard. I moan as my orgasm crashes through me, grinding my pussy against his face. Diego gentles his ministrations, and in a haze, I watch him slide a condom on his dick.

"Turn over," he whispers. "Get on all fours." I turn over but feel so uncomfortable. I have a big butt, and I don't want him to be grossed out. A surprised squeak leaves my mouth when his hand connects with my ass.

"What the hell!" I try to turn over, but he puts a hand on my back, staying me.

"Don't ever hide your body from me. You are gorgeous. Every. Inch. Of. You." He punctuates each word with a kiss to my back. I feel him spread my legs and feel the head of his cock nudge the inside of my thigh. Diego leans over my back and grabs my hands. "I want you to hold on to the headboard, keep your back arched, and I'll worry about your hips. You let go, and I stop—is that understood?"

Why do his words turn me on so much? "Yes, I understand." I wait with bated breath to see what he's going to do. I feel one hand grab my hip as the other moves between my legs. The head of his cock breeches my opening before slamming inside me to the hilt. I throw my head back, crying out. I feel stretched to the max, and if it's possible, he's deeper than ever before.

He again leans over my back, his lips grazing my ear. "Hold on tight."

I have a death grip on my headboard when he

169

rears back and then drives into me again. My breasts jiggle with each thrust, and I feel my orgasm build again. "Baby, you feel so good. You're so tight and wet." He stays planted deep inside me, and I shudder at the feel of his lips on my back. "Are you going to come soon? I can feel you getting more and more wet."

"Please," I moan. He reaches around my front, rubbing my clit until I shatter around him. Diego removes his fingers, grips my hips painfully, and begins to pound into me over and over until his movements become erratic and a throaty groan leaves him, vibrating against my back.

I let go of the headboard and collapse on the bed, Diego following me down. A whimper escapes as he pulls his softening cock from me. "I'll be right back. Don't move." I feel his weight lift off of me and the bed shift. I'm exhausted and can't move, so I close my eyes and wait for Diego to come back.

It wasn't hard to forgive him once he told me the truth. It was sweet of him to look out for me, but I meant what I said to him. I don't like being kept in the dark. My only hope is that if something like that happens again, he'll come to me and tell me what's going on.

The bed shifts as Diego climbs up and pulls me until I'm draped over his body. I place a kiss over his heart and snuggle into him. "This week was terrible," he says quietly. "I missed you. I hated seeing you and not being able to talk to you or not talking to you like I wanted to." He brushes my hair out of my face. "I don't like the way Clint watches you, the way he touches you."

I draw imaginary patterns on his chest. "I told him that I wasn't interested and to respect that, but yeah, he's been giving me the creeps. Truthfully, I don't think he'll do anything."

"Well I'm going to be watching him. I swear to you, Violet. If he gives any inclination that he's going to try something, you need to tell me."

"I promise I will." I reach up, kissing his lips.

He rolls us until he's on top of me, and it doesn't take us long before he's rolling another condom on and easing slowly into me. This man is going to kill me, but what a way to go.

Chapter Seventeen

Violet

I'm just pulling the cornbread out of the oven when I hear the buzzer, smiling to myself because that's Diego. It's been two weeks since the day that Diego came over and we talked. Since then, things have been going well. He's still worried about Penelope so we've had to be even sneakier than before. Sure, it gives our relationship an exciting element, but I'd give anything for us to be able to be out in the open.

I press the buzzer to open the door downstairs and open my door as I wait for Diego to come up. I'm only on the second floor, so it isn't long before I see him walking up the steps. "Hi."

"Hey, beautiful." He reaches me, and I can't help the smile on my face. When he reaches me, I throw my arms around his neck, kissing his lips hungrily. He's turned me into one giant, walking, talking hornball. Whenever he's around, all I want to do is have sex. Dani has assured me that there is nothing

172

wrong with me and that it's completely normal, and then she told me how jealous she was. Of course she said it to me with a smile on her face.

I reluctantly pull back. "Hi." Ugh...stupid. "I hope you're hungry; I made a ton."

He sniffs at the air. "That smell is heavenly. I'm starving."

I grab him a beer and set it in front of him at the table. Diego grabs me around the waist and pulls me toward him. "How did your test in your business class go?"

"I won't know until Monday, but I'm confident I aced it." I smile down at him because I'm getting all A's right now.

"My baby is brilliant." A shiver runs down my spine as he places his lips against my stomach. I love when he calls me baby and when he calls me his beautiful free spirit. The day I realized what he was saying to me in Spanish, I wanted to cry. Sometimes when we spend the night together, while we're snuggling in bed, he's been teaching me Spanish.

"Yes, I am." He lets me go so I can dish up our food. I decided to make him my favorite Brazilian dish, *Caruru de Camarao*. I carry our bowls over to the table and set them down before grabbing the cornbread and butter.

We both dig in, and I smile at the appreciative moans he's making as he shoves spoonful after spoonful into his mouth. I've never seen him like this. Usually he acts almost refined, but tonight he doesn't seem to care because he's chowing down like there is no tomorrow. I grab my cornbread and crumble it on top of my gumbo.

Once we're finished, I quickly clean up and am filling up the sink with water when Diego comes up behind me, wrapping his arms around my waist. "That was delicious." He moves my hair out of the way and kisses my neck. Goose bumps pop up all over my body every time he kisses me there.

"Thank you. It's a family recipe." I was ten when I helped my grandma make it for the first time. After that, it was always our thing. Then as my sisters got older, she did the same with them. I leave the dishes in the soapy water and let Diego pull me into the living room. We have yet to talk about the fact that the day in my apartment I had called Diego "professor." When it had happened the first time I had been mortified, but it seemed to fire him up. It felt natural to call him that at those moments.

We sit side by side on my sofa. He wraps his arm around my shoulders, pulling me into his side and kissing my forehead. "I wanted to ask. How's your mom doing?"

A sigh leaves my lips. "Things aren't great. My sister and I talked a couple of weeks ago, and she wants me to come home for a visit. I want to, but I've just wanted to wait until my tests were done. The only thing is if I go home now, I really don't think I can go home for Thanksgiving."

"Well, you need to do whatever is right for you. Baby, if you need help, I can help you."

I kiss his cheek and snuggle into him. "No, that's not the problem. I just don't want to miss classes, but then I feel bad because I know my family needs me."

He's quiet for a few minutes and then hugs me closer. "Book your flight. Go see your mom and grandma. As far as your classes go, I'll talk to your other professors and see if we can put together a packet for you of notes that you might miss. If you go next Friday, you'll only miss a review of the designs we've been working on."

"Diego, I don't want special treatment. Promise me you won't pull any favors or give me special treatment if I do this." I move so I'm on my knees next to him, grabbing his face in my hands. "Please promise me that you won't. I'll figure it out myself. Just like I'll take care of my job too." I've always been a pretty independent person.

"Baby, it's not pulling favors. It's what I'd do if one of my students were extremely ill or in the hospital. I don't want anyone getting behind."

I nod my head and snuggle into him, thoughts swirling around in my brain.

***

A whimper leaves my mouth as Diego pulls out of me, and I collapse on top of him. His hands stroke up and down my back, eliciting another moan from me. I could stay here in his arms forever.

After our talk earlier, I had been mentally exhausted and started dozing off on the sofa. I had barely remembered Diego asking me questions and couldn't tell you what they were, but when he had woken me up to go to bed, he showed me that he had bought me a gift card to Delta Airlines so I could fly home. I'd been stunned, flabbergasted—it was the nicest thing someone had ever done for me. He wanted to buy the ticket flat out, but he didn't want to step on my toes and knew I had to talk to my work.

I thanked him first with my mouth and then with my body…twice. The man has stamina, that's for sure. His recovery time seemed to be almost nonexistent. Of course, what did I know?

I'm so exhausted, both mentally and physically, that I can feel Diego move me around like a ragdoll, and then he whispers in my ear that he'll be right back. My eyes drift shut before I even feel the bed move.

The smell of toast wakes me. Rolling over, I see that Diego is up already. Gingerly, I crawl out of bed and then stretch my muscles. The delicious ache makes me smile, and my hand reaches up and covers up the bite mark on my neck.

I had been sitting astride him, and he was sitting up. I'd been so close to coming, and then he'd grabbed my hair at the base of my skull, wrenched my head to the side, and bit me right where my shoulder met my neck.

That had pushed me over the edge, and I had the most amazing orgasm. Crying out and digging my nails into his shoulders, I rocked my hips. Until he flipped me and began pounding into me with thrusts that bordered on painful, but it was a welcomed pain.

I shiver at the memory before picking up Diego's button-down shirt and slipping it on. Walking into the kitchen, I find Diego at my stove. He turns and gives me a smile that makes my breasts ache. "Good morning, *mi espíritu libre hermoso*. Did you sleep well?" I wrap my arms around his waist and kiss his neck. He moves my hair away from my neck and kisses his mark. "Does it make me a Neanderthal that I love seeing my mark on you?"

I pull back enough to look him in the eye. "No, it doesn't. I like knowing that it's there. It makes me ache to think about it." That last little bit comes out a whisper. I feel Diego drag his tongue up and over that spot before nipping at my earlobe.

"You shouldn't say those kinds of things to me, baby, because my cock is hard and we're out of condoms." A whimper leaves me as he whispers those words against my ear. See, he's turned me into a nympho. I reach in between us and cup his cock, which is in fact hard as a rock. Diego puts his hand over mine. "*Basta, bebé, por favor*. Stop baby, please. Are you on the pill?"

I shake my head no. "There was never really a reason to. I can get on it, if you want."

He cups my face in his hand. "You'd do that? Just so you know and so you don't worry, I was tested for STDs after Penelope."

I hadn't thought of STD testing too. "Of course. I'll make an appointment tomorrow." He kisses me before letting me go and grabbing me a cup of coffee.

While I sit drinking my coffee, I watch this beautiful man cook me breakfast, and a sense of calmness washes over me. I've always been a little high strung and nervous, but the more I'm around him, the more I feel normal, or what normal should feel like. Before Diego, some days I'd feel like I was crawling out of my skin, or if things didn't go the way I wanted, I'd have a meltdown. Sometimes crowds would make me edgy, and anytime my family traveled, I'd get crabby until we were actually on the road.

I hate having anxiety issues, but I've learned to deal with them, and for the most part my meds help. Shaking off those thoughts, I take a drink and watch Diego make us plates. I move to climb off of the counter, but Diego puts a hand on my thigh to stop me.

He forks up some eggs and holds them to my mouth. I look at him with a raised brow. "Let me. Please?" I open my mouth and moan around the best scrambled eggs I've ever eaten. While I chew, I watch him take a bite himself.

Back and forth he feeds himself and me eggs, bacon, and toast until both of our plates are empty. Why does it turn me on when he does that? We work side by side cleaning the kitchen even though I told him I would do it, and when that's all done, he kisses me before heading home to get ready for a meeting. I grab my phone and call my boss at the café to find out about getting a weekend off. She's so sweet and approves it right away.

Now all I need to do is book my flight.

***

My plane touches down, and I grab my bag from under the seat in front of me and place it on my lap. As I wait for us to reach the gate, the past two weeks come back to me. Things have been amazing between Diego and me. When I'm with him, I feel cherished, taken care of, but strong. I had been worried that he'd perceive me as weak because I let him take care of me sometimes, but like he said, I'm strong because I was letting him do it. At any time I could've said no, but so far I haven't.

School is going great—I'm getting all A's, and he was right, my teachers were understanding and gave me my assignments to complete while I was gone. I even bit the bullet and asked Clint to take notes for me, and he agreed unenthusiastically, and a part of me felt bad that I wasn't attracted to him because he was truly a nice guy…when he wasn't acting weird, which he had been.

Diego hadn't heard from that girl, either. The only thing that was bothering me—well, not so much bothering me, but maybe hurt me a little—was the fact that Dani told me the weekend before that there was a big charity event that was going to be happening in the next few months and that the faculty was putting it on, which meant that Diego was part of that, and he hadn't mentioned it once to me. I mean, I get why he didn't. It's not like he can take me as his date, but it still would've been nice to be asked. Dani did mention that students could buy tickets and we could always go together, which didn't sound half bad.

The seatbelt sign going off brings me back to now. Like cattle, I follow the herd as we make it off the plane and down the tarmac. I grab my suitcase and make my way to the rental car place. No one knows I'm coming, but I did text Lilah and asked what their plans were because I was having something delivered. I guess maybe Lilah might know, but she didn't let on.

During my hour drive home, I mentally prepare myself for my mom. I need to see with my own eyes what's going on. As soon as I hit the edge of town, I decide to stop by the cemetery to see my grandpa first. I drive my rental through the winding road until I reach the spot where he's buried. After throwing the car in park, I climb out and walk right to his tombstone.

On my knees, I reach out and touch his headstone. "Hi, Grampy. I came home for a short visit. Everyone's worried about Mom. I think she just misses you so much. We all miss you. I can't imagine you not being there when I graduate or when I get married someday. They want to sell the house, but I hate the idea of someone else living there or other kids up in the treehouse." I take a deep breath.

"I've met someone. He's amazing, and he treats me like I'm the greatest gift in the world. He's one of my professors, and we didn't plan this, but I think I'm starting to fall in love with him. I'm not sure if he feels the same, but he treats me like he does." I tell him about spending nights with him, cooking, talking, or just both of us reading. My grandpa hears about how Diego tries to help me when I'm studying, but I won't let him because I never want him to feel like I'm using him for grades.

I kiss his headstone before making my way back to my car and then toward my parents. Pulling up in front of the home I was born and raised in, I take a deep breath before climbing out of my car. I'm halfway up the driveway when I hear a scream from inside the house, and then my baby sister Daisy comes tearing out of the house. "Vi! What are you doing here?" I wrap my arms tight around her.

"I wanted to surprise you guys."

With our arms wrapped around each other, we head into the house. I'm greeted by my surprised-looking dad. "My baby girl. What are you doing home?" He picks me up, hugging me tight.

"I just missed you guys and wanted to see you. I thought surprising you might be nice. Where are Mom and Grandma?"

"They're sitting on the deck. They'll be so happy to see you." He wraps his arm around my shoulders, giving me a squeeze before we head outside. "Ladies, look what showed up on our doorstep. Should I send it away?"

They both turn, and their eyes widen before they jump out of their seats and run to me. "Oh, my baby girl is home!" My mom's voice holds so much joy it makes me smile. Her and Grandma both have their arms wrapped around me, but it isn't lost on me that my mom has lost some weight and she looks pale, but I keep my mouth shut and hug them tight.

Dad decides he wants to grill steaks, so I agree to ride with him to the store. I climb into his truck and wait until he backs out of the driveway. "Daddy, she looks terrible." My voice cracks.

He picks up my hand, giving it a squeeze. "Your mom's having a tough time, and she's just started talking to a grief counselor. I promise you she's improving." At the stoplight, he turns to me before turning back to the road. "Is that why you came home, baby?"

"Yeah, Lilah called me. She was worried. Why didn't you tell me how bad she was?"

"Honey, I know. Your mom made me promise not to talk to you about it. She didn't want you getting upset and coming home."

My dad pushes the cart through the grocery store as I grab stuff off of his list. We talk about school and my grades. I tell him about Dani and how she and I have spent a lot of time together.

"That's really great, honey. You're a genius like your old man." He gives me his signature cocky grin. "Will we get to meet Dani? I know how hard it is for you to make friends, so I'm guessing she's pretty great." Dad ends up buying enough food to have the rest of the family over. He instructed everyone to bring side dishes, and he'd take care of the meat.

Once we get back to the house, Dad tells Mom the plans, and I begin to straighten up the house alongside my grandma, who seems to be in a pretty good mood, or I should say she doesn't seem really sad like before, and honestly Grandma seems to be doing better than my mom. My sisters join us as we clean and then start helping to set up.

It isn't long before our family arrives. Joe comes to me immediately and scoops me up in his arms, hugging me tight. We talk for a bit before Carrington and her hubby, Damien, arrive with the twins. My uncle Luke, Carrington's dad, shoves everyone out of the way so he can get to his grandbabies. It's adorable, but I tell him I need some snuggle time and take little Shay from him to keep close.

Whenever my family gets together, it's loud and crazy, but we love each other. Abby and her daughter Natalie are the last ones to arrive, and unfortunately Ben's not with them because he's working. "Hey girlie, you look gorgeous." I pat her little belly and kiss her cheek.

"Thanks. I'm just glad that the morning sickness has finally stopped. What are you doing home? I was surprised when Mom called and said you were back."

I lean in close. "I was just a little worried about Mom, but Dad says she's talking to someone and getting better. So at least now I don't have to worry about her when I go back to school."

Abby leans into me. "Yeah, Mom and Aunt Bell have been making sure she's okay, both her and your grandma." I give her a big hug before we head out back to where everyone is gathered.

Chapter Eighteen

Diego

Over the speakers I hear them announce that Violet's flight has landed. I'm anxious to see my girl, and I've missed her more than I care to admit. It's hard to fathom that in the short time we've been together, I've fallen this hard for her. I crave her like a drug, and I need her. It's never happened to me before, but I feel like I'm falling in love with her.

Last night we talked, and it made me so happy to hear the relief in her voice that her mom was getting help for her grief and that my girl missed me too.

It takes fifteen minutes before I spot Violet. The moment our eyes meet, I expect the sappy love song to start as she gives me a huge smile and begins running to me. I meet her halfway and wrap her in my arms, kissing her with a tenderness I hope she can feel and showing her how much I missed her. She grips the front of my shirt as our kiss goes on and on, only to be interrupted by some asshole who shouts, "Get a room!" at us.

She pulls away first but gives me a big smile. "Hi." Violet's voice is no more than a whisper.

"Does it make me pathetic that I missed the fuck out of you?" I kiss her instead of letting her answer. Right now I need to get her home, to my room so I can bury myself between her thighs. "Let's get you out of here." I grab her bag with one hand and wrap my other arm around her shoulders.

On our way out to my car, she tells me about her weekend and then shows me pictures on her phone. There's one that warms something inside of me. It's Violet with a baby in her arm and an adorable little girl standing next to her. Images of Violet with a swollen belly fill my mind. The thought of children should scare me. I've never once thought about having kids. Don't get me wrong, I love my nieces and nephews...I just never thought about them for myself.

"Is that your cousin Cari's baby?"

"Yep, that's Ryder. His twin sister Shay was with her grandpa, who kept trying to hog both babies. The little girl next to me is Abby's adopted daughter, Natalie." She smiles wide as she looks at the picture and then at me. "It was great seeing everyone."

Violet stops me next to my car. "I don't know how I'll ever be able to repay you or thank you for what you did."

I cup her face. "It was no trouble. I knew how important it was to you to make sure your mom was okay." I kiss her one more time, and then I open the car door for her. "Did you have a chance to work on your homework while you were away?"

We make our way toward my place. I shouldn't presume that's where she wants to go, but she doesn't tell me to take her home.

"I have a little more to do. It won't bother you if I work on it for a little bit, will it?" I feel her eyes on me.

"Not at all. I'm sure you've got to be hungry, so I'll make us a late lunch while you work." She places her hand on my thigh and gives it a squeeze.

We get back to my place, and I bring her bag inside, taking it into my bedroom. When I come back out, I find her curled up on my chaise lounge with her laptop on her lap, her earbuds in, and a pen and notebook next to her. A smile graces my lips because when she's like this I could dance around naked and she wouldn't even notice.

In the kitchen, I pull out stuff to make her favorite sandwich: turkey, bacon, avocado, and tomato on honey wheat bread. Earlier today I stocked up on her favorite things: flavored creamer, tea, microwave popcorn, and cereal. I even bought the shampoo, conditioner, and body wash she uses. Maybe it's all part of my plan to get her to stay with me more.

I finish her sandwich and bring it out to her, stroking a hand down her hair and holding it up in front of her. She thanks me very loudly, and a laugh slips past my lips as I go into the kitchen to grab my sandwich. Outside on my patio, I grab my phone to call my mom.

"*Hola*, my baby boy. How are you?" I've decided to wait just a little bit longer before I tell my parents about Violet. I want to make sure we're solid before I say anything, because I know I'll need to convince them of how special Violet is and how different she is from any of the other women I dated.

"I'm good. Just looking forward to winter break so I can come home and see you. I'm almost done buying gifts, and then I'll get them wrapped so I can get them shipped to you." That's one of the hardest parts about living in another country.

"*Mijo*, I told you I could buy the gifts and wrap them here. It costs too much money to ship them." She says this every year, and it's honestly not that much money—I'm happy to do it.

"*Mamá,* I know you would, but I enjoy it. How's *papá?*" I'm very much like my father. My father is a good man, a hard worker—dedicated to the people he cares about. When he told me the story of how he fell for my mother, he said that they had dated for one week before he proposed, and that was only because he didn't want to scare her off by proposing too quickly. *Papá* said that things just clicked into place when they met.

That's exactly how it feels for me now with Violet. Things feel like they've clicked into place. Now I just need to figure out what to do about the whole forbidden thing.

"Your father is excellent, ornery as ever. He's at your brother's office helping him research a big case he's working on." My father's retired, but he loves to keep busy. He helps Jorge out a lot at the law firm.

"That's great." I turn toward the French doors

and see Violet in the kitchen. *"Mamá,* I have to go, but I'll call you next weekend."

"Okay, *mijo.* I love you." After hanging up, I step back inside the house and back to my girl.

***

"What'll happen if someone finds out about us?" Violet whispers. We're snuggled up naked in my bed. Her face is hidden against my neck and her arm's around my waist as I drag my fingers up and down her bare back, but her question makes me freeze.

To be honest, I haven't really looked into it. I guess that's one thing I should do. "I don't know, baby. I guess there's a chance that I could be fired or you could be expelled. Although I don't think anything would happen to you. I wouldn't let it." It's the truth. I'd let them fire me before I ever let her take the fall.

She pushes up until I can see her face clearly. "I don't want you to lose your job because of me. Maybe we should break this off." I move fast until I'm on top of her and between her legs.

Brushing her hair out of her face, I bend down to touch my lips to hers. "Do not worry about me. Tomorrow when I get to the office, I'll check the school policy and then we'll worry about it, okay? Promise me you won't worry about it now." I rub the pad of my thumb back and forth across her lower lip. "Violet, I'm serious. Promise me you're not going to worry about it."

Violet's eyes drift shut before she opens them

again. "Okay, I promise not to worry about it."

Our lips meet in the middle, and it's a slow glide. Her hands slide into my hair, and she deepens the kiss. I rock my now hard cock against her pussy and groan when I feel how wet she is. Violet moans into my mouth as I hit her clit over and over. All I would need to do is move down just a tiny bit and I would be at her opening. Fuck me, but I want to fuck her with nothing in between us.

She's on the pill now, but I've been waiting for her to give me the green light the past couple of weeks. I know she'll tell me when she's ready. I've never been bare inside a woman before, and it seems only fitting that the first time I am it would be with Violet. My lips travel down her neck, but I don't stop there. I keep going until I reach her luscious tits. Sucking one tip into my mouth, I bite it just enough to make her cry out.

I grab her hands and pin them to her sides as I move back and forth between both nipples. Her hands flex under mine, but I don't let go. Violet writhes beneath me, babbling incoherently. I want her to beg; I want to hear her beg me to fuck her. "What do you need, baby?"

Violet whimpers and thrusts her hips up but doesn't say it. I continue sucking and biting her nipples and sliding my dick through her wet folds. She moves her hips again, trying to impale herself on my cock, but I pull away. Violet moans, and I swear she just called me an asshole. I pull both of her arms up and above her head, shackling both wrists with one hand and wrapping the free one around her throat. "What was that?"

"Please!" she cries. I rub against her again.

"Please what? I want to hear you say it." I lower my mouth to her neck, nipping at her tender skin. "Tell me, Violet. What do you need?"

"Fuck me, you big jerkface!"

I bend down and kiss her before pulling away. "Do you want me to wear a condom? It's up to you, baby. I'll do whatever you want."

She doesn't even wait before whimpering, "Please, just fuck me. I can't take it."

That's all I need to hear before I'm thrusting inside heaven and burying myself to the hilt. She's so hot, wet, and tight. A groan rips from my throat as I feel her channel clamp down around me. I feel her whole body shudder, and I want nothing more than to beat on my chest. "You feel just like heaven," I tell her before slowly starting to move.

We move slowly together in a dance as old as time. I grab her thigh and pull it up higher on my hip, rolling my hips and loving the cries that leave her lips. We don't take our eyes off of each other as we move together. With every thrust inside her, I tilt my hips, hitting her sweet spot. Being inside her with nothing between us is one of the best feelings I've ever experienced.

That familiar tingle begins too soon, so I reach in between us and begin strumming her clit. Her cries become shouts as I feel her walls begin to flutter around me. "I need you to come, baby." I pinch her clit and thrust into her deep and hard, watching as her eyes start to roll back in her head, and she moans long and loud. She's so wet right now that with every thrust it makes a squelching sound.

I grab both of her thighs and push them until she's almost bent in half before I begin pounding repeatedly into her. I should be careful—I don't want to hurt her—but the desire to come deep inside her is overpowering. She reaches up and grabs my hair. That little bite of pain is enough to trigger my own orgasm, and I thrust erratically inside her. My balls draw up, and euphoria spreads through me as I empty myself inside of her with a groan.

When it finally stops, I collapse on top of her. She wraps her arms and legs around me, hugging me tight. The sound of our breathing is the only sound to be heard. When I finally gather my senses, I push up and look down at her. She's got a serene smile on her face, and I know it's there because of me.

"That was amazing," she says, her voice thick with exhaustion. I should clean her up, but I like the idea of my cum inside her.

I arrange us until she's draped over me with her head on my shoulder, and I feel her relax until her soft snores fill my room.

***

Scanning the policies, I find the one I'm looking for and start reading. My stomach turns violently as I continue to read. From what I gather, if a student and someone of authority enter in a relationship, then either the student needs to drop the class or leave that group. If someone files a complaint, then the department can launch a hearing. If the relationship is found out and neither participant made an attempt to switch classes or groups, then a full administrative hearing could be launched.

My eyes scan the rest of the policy, and it's not looking good for us. If she drops my class, then she'd have to wait until next semester to register for another class, which would screw up her GPA for now. A heavy sigh leaves my lips as I close that tab and then stare at my desk. If one of us left my class, then our relationship could be out in the open, but I can't ask that of her.

"What the hell do I do?" I whisper to myself.

Chapter Nineteen

Violet

Diego's acting weird. He's not giving me the cold shoulder like before, but he seems like he's on edge. I understand when we're in class that he has to treat me like any other student, but he has been snapping at all of us. So I've been doing what I do best—keeping my head down and just doing my work. Clint's being extra chatty today but not inappropriate…thank goodness, I'm glad my words got through to him.

The rest of the day, things are fine. My long weekend home didn't put me behind, so I've had no trouble staying up-to-date with assignments. Clint copied his notes for me and didn't try to finagle a study date out of me, for which I was grateful.

After my classes, I stop to meet Dani for lunch before I have to head to the library. I spot my friend sitting under a tree with her Kindle in her hand. I kick her foot when I reach her and move out of the way when she looks like she's going to kick my ass.

"Oh my God! I thought you were some jerk."

"Sorry, I didn't mean to scare you." I hold out my hand to help her stand up.

"No worries, I was just into this book. How was your weekend at home? How's your mom?" We haven't seen each other much over the past week. Between our classes, work, and other stuff, we've both been so busy.

"She's better. She looked sad and tired, but my dad's confident that the counselor she's talking to will help. My grandma seems to be doing well, but between my dad's parents and aunts and uncles, they're all keeping them busy or busier than usual. My dad says they're going to sell my grandparents' house." We get in line with our trays. "It makes me sick. I don't want anyone else living in that house, but I can't afford to buy it. We'll see what happens after the holidays."

We find a spot to sit in the corner, and Dani leans in. "How are things going with you guys?" It's so nice to have someone to talk to about this. Dani's been so sweet and supportive through it all.

"They're good, great actually, except something's wrong with him. I know he was going to look up the school's policies about...you know, but he hasn't mentioned anything to me. Hell, maybe he's just cranky."

"I still can't believe he paid for your ticket to fly home. That's so sweet."

"I know. I wanted to refuse, but he did it while I was sleeping, and I just desperately needed to get home. I'll pay him back eventually."

We finish eating and say goodbye as we head in

opposite directions. I reach the library and find Patty, the head librarian, behind the main desk.

"Hi, Violet. How are you, honey?" The older woman smiles at me as I come around the desk and put my bag under the counter.

"I'm good, Patty." I grab my cart and pull the books out of the return bin. I move through the library putting books away and straightening the shelves.

I'm back in the corner when I feel someone come up behind me. Turning around, I find Clint standing there. "Um...hey, Clint. What's up?" There's a weird vibe coming off of him. It sucks because I'm in a spot that I can't get away from him. "Can you please back away? You're making me uncomfortable."

"I just have something I wanted to show you." He pulls out his phone, swipes his finger a few times, and then sticks it in my face.

My stomach sinks when I see it's clearly the airport. My hands begin to tremble when Diego appears on the screen. I watch as a wide smile stretches across his lips, and then he's on the move. The camera follows as we meet in the middle and our lips touch. If this had been any other situation, I might have melted seeing this video, but right now I want to vomit.

I open my mouth to speak, but Clint moves and puts his fingers over my mouth. "So that's why he stopped giving you a hard time. You know, I couldn't figure out what was going on at first, but then I started to notice the way you looked at him, the way he watched you." He leans in even closer, and I can feel his hot breath on my ear. "Are you fucking him? Do you fuck all of your teachers for grades?" My hand whips out to slap him, but he swats it away.

"No, I'm not sleeping with anyone for anything." I swallow down the bile that rises in my throat.

"Don't. Lie. To. Me. You don't think I've followed you. If you're not fucking him, then why have you spent the night at his house?" I try to speak, but he stops me. "I don't want to hear any more of your bullshit stories. I'm going to need some time to decide what I want to do with this knowledge. Until then, I don't want you to see him."

"You can't tell me what to do. I'll come clean about our relationship. I'll tell them I pushed for it and that I wouldn't let him say no." My heart hammers in my chest. Sweat runs down my back.

"Nah, that won't work. Does this look like you had to do much pushing?" Again, he shows me his phone. I don't know when it was taken, but we're in Diego's car and he's holding my face in his hands and he's kissing me with vigor. What do I do? Despair fills me because it would kill me if he lost his job because of me.

He begins to back away, and I let out a sigh of relief that is short lived when he approaches me again. "Actually, I know what I want. You're going to sleep with me. If you say no, then that video and those pictures will be posted everywhere. He'll lose his job and you'll get kicked out of school." Tears fill my eyes. "I will, however, give you time to think about it. How about after Thanksgiving break?

Will that work for you, sweetheart?"

"Do I have choice?"

"Nope, not really. By the way, you and I are going to start spending more 'quality' time together. We'll start with coffee tomorrow. Nine a.m. at The Drawing Board. Be there or else." I hold my body stiff as a board as he leans in and kisses my cheek. As soon as he disappears, the tears that I'd tried to hold at bay begin to spill down my cheeks. I wipe my face off with the back of my hand and take a deep breath.

Patty sees me walk up. "Honey, are you okay?"

I shake my head. "I don't feel very good. Is it okay if I go home?"

"Of course. Do you want a ride?"

I grab my bag and put it across my body. "No, but thank you. I'll be okay." I practically run across campus to head back to my apartment. Once I'm safely inside, I head into the bathroom, grab my bottle of Ativan, and shake one pill out of the bottle. I swallow it dry and then stare at myself in the mirror. My eyes are glassy and bloodshot. Red splotches cover my face. I throw my hair up into a ponytail and then splash cold water on my face.

In my bedroom, I lie down on my bed and wait impatiently for my Ativan to kick in. What am I going to do? I can't sleep with Clint. I'm in love with Diego, but I can't let him lose his job because of me. He loves teaching. Maybe I'll drop his class. It'll screw up my GPA, but at this point, I don't care. Should I tell Diego? No...if I do, he could go after Clint and get in more trouble.

Luckily, I feel my pill begin to kick in and let

sleep take me under.

Bam, bam, bam. A pounding somewhere wakes me with a start. It's completely dark in my apartment. My clock says it's nine thirty. *Bam, bam, bam.* It takes a second to realize that the pounding is coming from my door. I stumble out into the hall. My legs feel wobbly as I move toward the door. I look through the peephole and see Diego on the other side. Earlier today comes back to me, and my eyes fill with tears again.

"Violet, I can hear you. Open the door, baby." I take a deep breath and do what he asks. He takes one look at me and rushes inside. "What happened?"

I shake my head and turn away from him, making my way back down the hall and into my bedroom. The sound of the door shutting echoes through the apartment, and then he's in my bedroom. I ignore him, crawling back into bed and pulling the blankets over my head. The sound of clothes rustling can be heard, and then the covers are lifted. I try to roll away from him, but he halts me and rolls me back toward him.

"Baby, what is going on?" He brushes my hair out of my face.

Tears leak from my eyes, but I quickly brush them away. "N-Nothing."

"It doesn't look like nothing, baby. Please tell me."

I take a deep breath, trying to think of anything I can tell him, other than the truth. There's no telling what he'd do if he knew what Clint was trying to do. I need to come up with a plan on my own. I

198

don't like lying, but for now it's for his own good. "My mom called me today, and they're selling my grandparents' home. It just makes me sad because I have so many wonderful memories in that house. Hell, the treehouse I helped build is in the backyard. I don't know, I just really thought they'd keep it."

"I'm sorry, baby." He wraps his arms around me and hugs me close. "I know how much building that treehouse with your grandfather meant to you."

I snuggle into him, hating the fact that I just lied to him.

***

Tomorrow I fly home for Thanksgiving break, and to be honest, I'm freaking the fuck out. Clint had given me until after Thanksgiving to give him my answer about sleeping with him.

Over the past two weeks, I've been subjected to his incessant flirting, study "dates," and pretending that things have been hunky dory. Diego hasn't caught on, thank God, but the deadline is in just a few days, and I will never sleep with Clint. Especially knowing that Diego is in love with me.

Last week, Diego had taken me to Shreveport, where we stayed in the most charming bed and breakfast. It was one of those places that you'd see in a magazine or on a TV show. Being far away from school, we didn't have to hide our relationship, and it was refreshing. As we walked around doing some sightseeing, we got to hold hands, and he even kissed me right out in the open. We took tons of pictures to remember our time there.

It was while we were eating at the coolest little seafood shack that Diego had grabbed my hand and pulled me closer to him. "You're so beautiful. I'm so happy when I'm with you." A part of me felt nothing but happiness, but another part of me felt nothing but fear—fear of the unknown.

"I feel the same." After we had finished eating, we went for a walk along the Red River. His arm had been around my shoulders, hugging me close. We walked out onto a little pier, and he turned me toward him.

He cupped my face with his hands. "I'm in love with you, Violet Carmichael." Tears began to fall as I leaned in and touched my lips to his.

"I'm in love with you too, Diego Torres." After that, he had taken me back to our room at the bed and breakfast and made love to me slowly all night long. It had been easy to forget about Clint during that weekend, but that asshole was never far from my thoughts.

Ugh, of course Clint ruins the happy thoughts running through my mind now. I've spent more time with him than I ever wanted to. He makes me meet him for coffee all of the time. He tried to add dinners, but I had to beg and plead for him not to. Diego would start to suspect something if I spent more of my free time with Clint. I've missed the deadline to officially drop Diego's class, but I can withdraw from it. I just won't get credit for it and will have to take it again.

I'm packing my bag when I get a text from Dani telling me she's coming over. I've told her a little about what's going on, and she was ready to go hunt down Clint and kick his ass. She demanded that I tell Diego, but I couldn't because I was afraid of how he'd react.

A short time later, my buzzer sounds, and I press the button to let Dani in. I stand at the top of the stairs and smile when I see her trucking up the stairs. "Hey, girl!" I call out.

"Hey." She gives me a hug before stepping into my apartment. "Sorry to just stop by, but I wanted to see if you told Diego about Clint yet?"

"No, I wanted to wait until I withdrew from his class. I know Diego will go after Clint, and that's the last thing I want." My eyes fill with tears. "When I go home, I'm telling my parents what's going on just in case I get kicked out of school. Why did this get so fucked up? I love him, Dani, and I feel like when he finds out what happened, he's going to break things off."

Dani wraps her arms around me. "Hey, no negative thinking. I bet you'd be surprised by his reaction."

I wipe my tears away and nod, but I still don't feel good about it. Dani hugs me one more time before she leaves. I sit heavily on my sofa and pray that I wake up from this nightmare.

Chapter Twenty

Diego

Most staff and students are gone already or are getting ready to leave. That's one bad thing about having no family around, because it'll be just me for Thanksgiving. If I truly had my wish, I'd be spending it with Violet, but maybe next year. Something's going on with her, and it's more than just being upset about her grandparents' home being sold. Every now and then I catch her staring at me with sad eyes.

A part of me thinks that there is something going on with her and Clint, but then I remind myself that it's the dumbest thought I've ever had. We love each other, we're solid, and when I took her to the airport this morning, she hugged me so tight and cried. As I watched her walk away, I felt like I was watching her walk away for good, which made me feel unsettled.

I'm in the middle of grading a pop quiz I gave my classes yesterday when there's a knock on my office door. I look up and find a petite blonde standing there. She looks familiar, but I can't place where I've seen her.

"Can I help you?"

"Professor Torres, I'm sorry to bother you, but I'm Dani. I'm a friend of Violet's."

I stand up. "Please, come in. Can you shut the door?"

She sits down across from me and looks nervous. "I'm sorry to just come in here unannounced, but there's something that you should know. I know about you and Violet." My body locks up tight.

"Okay," I say very slowly. "What can I do for you, Dani?"

"Sir, there's a student in your class who is blackmailing Violet." She takes a deep breath. "A guy named Clint has seen the two of you together and showed Violet pictures and a video that prove that. He told her that he wants to sleep with her, and if she doesn't, then he's sharing the evidence with everyone so you get fired and she gets kicked out of school. He told her that she had until after this break to decide. Just so you know, she's planning on withdrawing from your class."

I'm speechless and fucking pissed right now. "Why didn't she tell me?"

"She was afraid you'd go after Clint and get into trouble. I think she's worried you're going to hate her. She loves you, and I think she's afraid she's going to lose you."

I pinch the bridge of my nose and sigh. "I appreciate you coming and telling me this. I knew something was going on with her."

"I saw her yesterday, and she got really upset. She plans on telling her parents what's going on. Especially since she's withdrawing from your class."

What the fuck? I was hoping that I could be with her when she told her parents. Facing her father like a man and telling him I was in love with his daughter was important to me. Was the guy going to kick my ass? Probably, but I'd prove to him that I was good for his daughter and that I could take care of her. I know what I need to do.

"Dani, I appreciate you stopping by and telling me this."

"No problem. I'm just glad that I decided to come see you. I love Violet, and I just hate the fact that Clint, the shit head, is messing with her." Dani stands up. "I don't think I need to tell you that Violet's one of a kind. Sure, I haven't known her long, but I've got a good sense about these things. If you hurt her, I'll kill you." She winks at me before disappearing from my office.

I jump on my computer and book a flight to get me to Violet. My credit card cries as I pay for it. A holiday weekend and no notice, and I'm paying a lot of money for that ticket, but it's worth it. I just need her—I need to hold her and let her know we'll deal with this together.

***

As my plane lands in Charleston, I take a deep breath and shake out the tension in my shoulders. Last night I had called my parents and finally told them about Violet. My mother was thrilled until I told her the rest of the details, and by the rest of the details I mean that Violet is my student and that she's a lot younger. For about twenty minutes, she screamed and cried at me until my father finally got on the phone.

"Son, do you know what you're doing? You could lose your job because of this. Is she worth it? Is she worth a career you've worked so hard for?"

"You told me that when you met Mom that you knew she was it for you. That's how I feel about Violet. She's so smart and talented. She built a treehouse with her dad and grandfather when she was just sixteen, and I've seen it—it's still in just as good a shape as when they built it. I tried to fight my feelings for her, but I just couldn't."

"Well sometimes, son, we have to follow our hearts. If she's worth it, then go for it. I'll support you, and your *mamá* will come around. Let's face it—you haven't had the best luck with women, or at least picked the right ones. We'll want to meet her and see for ourselves how wonderful she is."

After I hung up, I emailed the chancellor to disclose my consensual relationship with Violet and that her plan was to withdraw from my class. I told him that whatever was decided I would accept, whether it's losing my job, resigning, or suspension. I know he's not going to see it until after break, so there is no use worrying about it until Monday.

I disembark from the plane, making my way toward the car rental place. Once I'm on the road, I'm anxious to get to Violet and get the unpleasantness out of the way first. Plus, I just want to make sure that she's okay. I'm still not sure how to handle Clint, because he could still release the video and pictures no matter what happens, and that could be a major embarrassment for Violet.

According to the GPS, I'm only twenty minutes out, so I pull over and send her a quick text.

Diego: Hey baby. I just wanted to see what you're doing?

She answers me back almost immediately.

Violet: Hey, we're getting ready to go to my Uncle Dylan and Aunt JoJo's house. I hate that you're alone today.

God, I love her. I don't answer her back, but I jump back on the road and head toward her parents' house.

***

Violet

I'm in my sister Daisy's room finishing getting dressed when there's a knock on the door. "Are you decent?" my dad says through the door.

"Yeah, come on in." He steps in the bedroom. My dad looks so handsome in his blue button-up shirt and dress pants. When I was younger, girls at school used to always comment on how hot my dad was, which was gross and I hated hearing it, but the guys always talked about my mom. "What's up,

Dad?"

He sits down on the edge of Daisy's bed. "Are you okay? You seem really distracted."

"I'm fine. There is something I need to talk to you guys about, but that can wait until later."

"Sweetheart, are you sure? We can talk now."

"I'm sure, Dad. It's seriously not a big deal. I just want to talk to you guys about some stuff. I promise you that I'm okay." I change the subject. "Mom seems to be doing a lot better."

He wraps his arm around my shoulders, hugs me to his side, and kisses my forehead. "She is. It makes my heart happy to see your mama smile again. I actually heard her singing while she was editing some pictures the other day." My mom has always been a singer, so I know it's a good thing if she is singing again.

"That's great."

I promise him that we'll talk tomorrow, and I watch him leave. My stomach starts to hurt. I already know that he's going to be disappointed in me, but how can he fault me for how I feel? I know he and Mom didn't have the easiest start, but he always knew that she was the one for him. I'm hoping that he'll understand that.

This morning I had woken up to a text from Clint telling me,

Four days.

I immediately ran into the bathroom and got sick. Thanks to that asshole, I've been using my Ativan a lot more than I'd like. My nerves are honestly shot. Every day I've had to pretend that things are fine. It's getting harder and harder to do, and I can only hope and pray that when I tell my parents and withdraw from the class that things will go back to normal.

I hear the doorbell chime and am slipping my shoes on when I hear voices, loud ones coming from the living room.

"Are you stalking my daughter? Because this isn't the first time you've shown up out of the blue. What do you want from her?" I quickly make my way down the hall, and Diego is standing in the living room.

"What are you doing here?" I ignore the questioning looks from my family and the death glare that my dad is giving him.

He ignores them too and grabs my hand. "I need to talk to you." I can't ignore his pleading tone and drag him out of the front door.

My dad follows behind us. "Violet, what is going on?" He moves to stand in front of us. "Explain to me why one of your professors showed up not once but twice in your hometown, where I'm guessing he does not live."

"Sir, I'm happy to explain things to you, but first I just want a moment to discuss something with Violet." Dad looks at Diego like he's ready to strike him. I move to get in between them.

"Dad, let me talk to Diego, and then we'll talk, okay?" Oh shit, calling Diego by his first name probably wasn't the best idea. My dad's face turns a scary shade of red, and he goes to move me out of the way. "Daddy, don't."

"Jesus Christ! You're sleeping with him." I can't even look him in the eye right now. "He's your fucking teacher." He looks at Diego over my shoulder. "You touched my daughter? One of your students?"

My mom comes rushing out, followed by my sisters, who stay on the steps. My dad completely ignores her. "Daddy, I love him."

In a flurry of motion, I'm moved out of the way, and my dad punches Diego in the face. Diego stumbles back but doesn't go after him—he just takes it. My dad moves toward him again, ready to strike, but my mom jumps in front of him.

"Dustin, stop." She looks at me, disappointment written all over her face. "Violet, get him out of here until your dad calms down."

Tears cloud my vision as I grab Diego's hand and lead him to what I suspect is his rental car. The keys are in it, and I turn it on. I look at my childhood home and find my dad standing on the steps staring at us. Diego grabs a shirt out of his bag in the backseat and holds it to his bleeding nose.

He tells me where he made a reservation so we head to the hotel. Both of us are silent, and the vibe in the car is heavy. Once we reach the hotel, he gives me his credit card, and I check him in. We stand side by side as we ride up the elevator to his room. Once inside, I go into the bathroom to wet a washcloth and then start wiping the blood off of his face. His cheek is swollen but his nose isn't, so I don't think it's broken.

"I'm going to get some ice." I get up and grab the bucket before heading out into the hall. I reach the ice machine and lean against the wall. Tears slide down my face—I knew this wasn't going to go well, but I didn't expect it to go downhill so fast. I've never seen my dad like that, and Mom looked so upset with me. With quick hands I wipe the tears away, fill the bucket, and head back to Diego's room.

I take a deep breath and step back inside. Diego hasn't moved from his spot on the little sofa. In the bathroom, I grab a hand towel and then fill it with ice. I grip his chin and tip his face up. His expression is blank, and my stomach sinks. He winces as I hold the ice to his face. Neither of us speaks, but the tension is so thick you could cut it with a knife.

My insides quake, but I don't let it show. This wasn't supposed to be how this all went. In my mind, it went a lot differently. In my imagination did I picture it going well with my dad? No, but I didn't think it would end in my dad punching someone.

I can't take the silence any longer. "Why are you here?" My voice is nothing but a whisper.

With bated breath, I wait for him to answer me. With a sigh, he finally speaks. "I came to break things off with you. I felt it was better to do it in person and to do it right away. I'm sorry to ruin your Thanksgiving, but I didn't want to wait any longer. Penelope and I are going to give it another go." If it's possible to feel your heart breaking, I can feel mine doing it right now, but I won't let him see it happen. "I'm flying out tonight. You should probably get going; I don't want you to miss out on your family time."

Numbly, I drop the towel in front of him. On shaky legs, I stand up and, without looking at him, walk out of his room. Right before getting in the elevator, I swear I hear something slam, but I probably imagined it.

Chapter Twenty-One

Dustin

Stacy holds ice on my knuckles, and I wince at first because of the cold. It's been a long time since I've lost my cool like that. When I had opened the door and found her professor standing there, a sick feeling filled my gut. I know I can't expect my girls to be innocent forever, and Violet had always had issues when it came to men. Knowing that the son of a bitch defiled my daughter sits like a rock in my gut. I'd always imagined that Violet would be the innocent one until she got married.

I can only imagine what he said and did to con my daughter into bed. If it wasn't a holiday, I'd call the school right now and lodge a complaint against him, but it'd only hurt Violet. I look behind me, and Lilah and Daisy are both watching me with wary eyes from the sofa. Thank God Stacy's mom had

212

already gone to my parents' house. I'm surprised one of our neighbors didn't call the cops, but trees surround our house so hopefully it shielded us.

"Hold that there and I'll get you some ibuprofen." My beautiful wife kisses my cheek before disappearing down the hall.

"Is Vi coming back?" Daisy asks with tears in her eyes. I sit down between my two daughters and wrap my arms around their shoulders.

"I'll call her and make sure she comes back." I grab my phone out of my pocket, thumb through the contacts, and put it to my ear. Unfortunately, I can hear it ringing from the kitchen. "Shit." I stand up as Stacy comes back into the living room with a bottle of ibuprofen. "Violet left her phone. Should we head to my parents and assume she's going to show up there?"

She wraps her arms around my waist, and her flowery scent wraps around me, calming me. "She'll show up there. We should go. Here, take these." I shake a couple of pills into my hand and grab a glass of water to swallow them down.

"Okay guys, let's go." We all make our way outside, and I hope Violet shows up.

***

I check my phone for the hundredth time, and she still hasn't shown up yet. Guilt plagues me as I see the concern on my wife and daughters' faces. There were a million other ways I could've handled the situation, but all I could see in my head was that piece of shit defiling her, taking advantage of her.

Deep down I know he didn't. My girl is smart—she wouldn't let anyone play her.

After carrying my plate into the kitchen and throwing it into the garbage, I slip out the back door into my parents' backyard. I lean against the railing and stare out at nothing. Where is she? Why did I hit him? I'm not a violent person.

"What's going on?" I turn to find my brother and brother-in-law/best friend standing behind me, concern etched on both of their faces. "Why isn't Violet here, and why do you all look like someone died?" my brother Dylan asks.

I lay it all out, and when I say I lay it out, I mean I tell them everything—Violet finding out about what happened to her mom, the panic attacks thinking the guy who tried to kill her mom was her dad, her habitual shyness around guys, and then about Diego. "I punched him in the front yard in front of my wife and daughters. Who does that?"

"Dustin, you don't think I'd do the same thing for one of my girls? I can guarantee Luke would do the same thing for Care Bear. You and Violet have always shared a special bond, so of course you're going to be overprotective. That girl has always wore her heart on her sleeve since she was itty bity." Dylan grabs my shoulder.

"I'm going to run by the house and see if she's there. Tell Stacy I'll be back." They nod, and I'm thankful my keys are still in my pocket so I don't have to explain what's going on.

I pull into the driveway, and after a quick run through, it's obvious she's not here. Of course I don't have any clue where *he's* staying and if Violet is even still with him, but something tells me if things were okay she would've shown up at her grandparents'.

Where could she be? It hits me, and I run back outside and hop in my car, driving across town to my mother-in-law's house. I park in front of the house and then walk around the side until I reach the tree.

The day we finished building this, I had been filled with so much pride. My girl was out here every day working even after she broke her finger. She never gave up. I climb up the ladder and peek inside. My heart shatters at the sight in front of me. My beautiful daughter is staring blindly at the wall with tears running down her face.

I have to crawl through the treehouse to get to her. She still hasn't acknowledged me. I wrap my arms around her and listen as she begins to sob in my arms. As she cries, I rock her back and forth. She's breaking my heart right now. "Baby girl, I'm so sorry I hit him. Please don't hate me."

"I-I don't h-hate y-y-you," she stutters out. "He br-broke up with me. He told me he loved me and then told me he's getting back with his ex-girlfriend." Violet clutches my shirt. "Why does it hurt so much? I thought he was the one."

I want nothing more than to find that bastard and punch him again. Instead, I keep holding my girl and trying to comfort her.

A while later she's still crying but calmed down enough that I can get her out of here and home. Before we pull away from the house, I shoot my wife a text telling her that I'll be there to pick them up and if they could make a plate for Violet to eat when she's up for it. Stacy asks me what happened, but I tell her we'll talk about it later.

Stacy: Okay baby, I love you. Kiss our girl for me.

Dustin: I love you, too.

***

Diego

I let myself into my home and throw my bag across the room. Yesterday I watched the beautiful light go out in Violet's eyes, and it was my entire fault. I had every intention of telling her I knew about Clint and the blackmail, I was going to my boss to disclose our consensual relationship, and that more than likely she'd have to withdraw from my class. It was all planned out, and then I showed up at her parents' house.

Her dad was so pissed, and Violet looked so hurt. I did the right thing breaking things off with her. I did. She deserves to fall in love with someone her own age and someone who wouldn't jeopardize her future like I would. Does that make it hurt any less? No, not at all.

I grab my bottle of bourbon and pour a generous amount in a tumbler. I drink it down in two swallows before pouring more into my glass and drinking that down. Taking my glass with me, I step into my bedroom, and Violet's scent still lingers. I walk over to my bed, pick up her nightgown, and bring the silky fabric up to my face. It smells like her lotion, citrusy and warm.

I've never seen the light go out in someone's eyes before, and it was so hard to just sit there and then to tell her I was with Penelope. It had to go down that way. I had to make her hate me. "Mission accomplished, idiot," I mutter to myself. Before I leave my bedroom, I lay her nightgown on my pillow. My bathroom counter is cluttered with her toiletries, shampoo, conditioner, and what not. I need to stop torturing myself.

I grab the bottle of bourbon off of my kitchen counter and carry it outside where I plan on getting very, very wasted.

***

After logging into my computer in my office, I pull up my emails—nothing from the head of the school yet. I shoot him another email informing him that the relationship is over, but if he still needed to meet, I would make myself available for him. My plan is to talk to him but also let him know that I'll be kicking Clint out of my class for blackmailing another student for sex.

I'm not sure how I'll be able to keep myself from saying anything to him, but I know I can't. I need to be professional and act like nothing is wrong when all I want to do is pummel his face. There hasn't been any notification that Violet has withdrawn from my class yet, and I honestly don't know if she'll be there today. With a sigh, I stand up and grab the papers off of my desk and head to my class.

The room is empty when I arrive, and I set my stuff down on my desk and have a seat. I won't lie—I'm watching the door like a hawk. One by one, my students enter. I politely ask about their Thanksgiving break and nod appropriately while they talk. I move back toward my desk when that little shit Clint walks in. He gives me a nod and then sits down in his chair. It's time for class to start, and Violet's chair is empty. I notice that Clint notices too, and then he looks at me with a raised brow. I ignore him and teach my lesson.

After class, I check my emails and see one from Chancellor Williams letting me know that he's available at eleven. I let him know that I'll be there. I'm scanning the rest of my emails when I see the one that I've been dreading from the registrar's office. It informs me that Violet Carmichael has withdrawn from my class. I close my eyes as a pain I've never experienced before pierces my chest.

When it's time to meet the chancellor, I head across campus. I reach the building and step inside. My footsteps echo through hall, and I feel like I'm heading to my execution. Of course that's an exaggeration, but a sense of foreboding fills me. I spot his secretary up ahead, and she smiles as I approach.

"Good afternoon, Professor Torres. He said you could head on in." I give her a smile and nod before I knock on the door and step inside.

Chancellor Williams is a short, round man with short, gray hair. He's always been a nice man but a stickler for the rules. "Thanks for seeing me, Chancellor."

He comes around his desk to shake my hand. "Please call me Tom. Can I get you some water or coffee?"

"No thank you, I'm good."

"Okay, let's get down to business. This relationship, it's over?"

"Yes sir, I ended it this weekend. She's also withdrawn from my class. I'm prepared to take whatever punishment you want to give me."

Tom doesn't say anything at first. I keep my face neutral and don't let him see me freaking out.

"Well, since the relationship is over, there isn't much we need to do. Thank you for your honesty about the situation. Not to change the subject, but how are the donations coming for the masquerade ball?" I don't answer right away, because to be honest, I'm dumbstruck that he basically did nothing in regards to my relationship with Violet. "Diego?"

"Yes, sorry. We've got lots of great items. We managed to get some package deals too—overnight stays, dinner, and dancing. A lot of local businesses were happy to donate. How is everything else coming along?"

"Everything is pretty much lined up and ready to go. Tickets are almost sold out."

"That's great." It hits me I forgot to mention Clint. "There is something else that I wanted to talk to you about. Another student discovered our relationship and is trying to blackmail Ms. Carmichael into having sex with him—if she doesn't, he said he was going to let everyone know what's going on…or what *was* going on."

"Really? What's the name of the student?" I tell him, and he informs me that he'll want to speak to Violet about it.

"Well, I'll be getting back to you about it. This will more than likely warrant disciplinary action. I'll be in touch." That makes me feel a little bit better about things. Maybe the little asshole will get kicked out of school.

This was just another reason why we shouldn't be together. Maybe if I keep saying it enough, I'll finally believe it.

Chapter Twenty-Two

Violet

It's been a week since Diego broke my heart. Things have been okay, but I still hurt; I still cry when I think about him. I don't know why I thought I'd be able to turn my feelings off, because I haven't been able to. I love him—I love him even though he shattered me. I've only seen him a couple of times since it happened, and he's ignored me. Withdrawing from his class was an easy decision. I didn't want to see him every day and know that he was with someone else. Especially that vile girl, but what did I expect? Before him, I'd barely kissed a guy and certainly had no relationship experience.

She was probably perfect, but I guess as long as she makes him happy, that's all that really matters.

When I told Dani about the breakup, she got pissed. It turns out that she went to him after I'd already gone home and told him about Clint. She was under the impression that he was coming to me to tell me he knew and to figure things out, not break things off. It didn't matter anymore. It was over, and I was never going to trust another man ever again.

I'm on way across campus to talk to the chancellor. I have no clue about what—well, maybe it's about Diego; I just hope that he's not there. I don't think I could handle seeing him right now.

Once I reach his office, his secretary leads me inside. Diego is sitting in a chair when I walk in, but he stands up along with the chancellor. Chancellor Williams comes around the desk and holds his hand out. "Ms. Carmichael, thank you for coming in. Please have a seat."

I avoid looking at Diego even though I can feel his eyes on me. Can he see the pain I feel? Does he even care? Probably not since he had no problem breaking up with me on Thanksgiving while I was visiting my parents.

"Ms. Carmichael, I've called you in because I've recently learned that another student has blackmailed you or has tried to blackmail you about your relationship with Professor Torres. I understand that the relationship is over, but blackmail is serious and something we will not tolerate. I just wanted you to be aware that we'll be suspending Clint Webster, and he'll have to appear in front of the disciplinary committee where they'll decide whether he can continue his education here or not. I do ask that you give a statement to the committee of what exactly transpired between you and Mr. Webster. Are you okay with that?"

"Y-Yes, sir. Just let me know when. Is it okay if I go? I have to get to the library." I don't really, but I need to get out of here.

"Of course. Again, thank you for coming in, and I'm sorry this happened to you. This is certainly something that won't be tolerated."

"Um…he has pictures and a video of Professor Torres and me together. There is a chance he'll do something with them. They're n-not bad, but it's clear in them that we're together, or were together."

"Unfortunately, we won't be able to stop him from releasing anything, but I assure you if he does, we'll do our best to remove it or delete it immediately."

"I understand—I just wanted you to be aware that he could do that. I'm sure he's going to." I stand up, and they both follow suit, but I avoid Diego's eyes. His cologne wafts toward me, and my body comes alive. Stupid body.

"We'll be in touch."

"Okay. Thank you, Chancellor Williams. Have a good day." I skirt by Diego, and thankfully my body doesn't brush by his.

I hightail it out of the building and head toward my apartment when I hear him. He's calling my name. I move faster, and it isn't long before he's grabbing my arm and stopping me. He turns me until we're facing each other, but I look anywhere but at him.

"Violet, look at me, please." Like a petulant child, I shake my head. "I made a mistake."

"A mistake?"

"Can we go somewhere and talk?" I finally look at him, and I'm a little taken aback. He looks about as bad as I do. His olive skin is a little paler than usual. He's got dark bags under his eyes. Diego just looks tired. Of course this was what he wanted, not me.

I sigh. "What's there to talk about? You said all you needed to say last week. Where's Penelope? Getting her talons painted? Staring at herself in a mirror?" I turn to walk away, but he grabs my arm again. Tears blur my vision. "Please, let me go."

He grabs me by my face. I try to pull back because we're out in the open, but he doesn't let go. "I made a mistake. I thought I was doing the right thing by you. I was trying to make things easier for you. God, this got so screwed up. I came to see you to tell you I knew about Clint, but then I saw the look on your father's face, and then he hit me, which I deserved, and you looked so sad, and it hit me that I should let you go to find someone your own age. I lied about being back with Penelope. I knew if I told you I was back with her that it would keep you from wanting to be with me."

I'm baffled right now. Instead of asking me what I wanted, he took that decision away from me. "You hurt me. You lied to me, and why? Because you couldn't talk to me about everything? I love you so much, and you broke my heart." Great, I'm crying.

"I know, baby. I'm so, so sorry. I love you, *mi amor*. Please, can we go somewhere and talk?"

What could it hurt? Well, okay, it could hurt me, but I don't think I could possibly hurt more than I'm already hurting. "Yes, okay. My place is closer." He tilts my face up and kisses my forehead.

Diego backs up and smiles at me before grabbing my hand and leading me through campus. I look around, worried that people are watching us, but honestly no one is paying us any mind. Neither of us says anything as we walk hand in hand toward my apartment. When we reach it, he takes my keys and lets us in. He follows me into the kitchen. "Do you want some tea?"

I feel his body heat as he comes up behind me. "No baby, I don't." He cages me in. "I want you to forgive me. Forgive me for breaking your heart, for hurting you and lying. I thought I was helping; I thought I was doing the right thing." Diego's arms wrap around my waist.

"What about school? What about your job?" I turn around so we're facing each other. He reaches up with one hand and cups my cheek.

"As long as I'm not teaching you, there is nothing that says that we can't be in a relationship. I'll just have to disclose it to the chancellor, but before you got there today, I told him since you were no longer my student that I was going to try and win you back." Warmth settles in my belly as he strokes my cheek. "Can you forgive me for hurting you?"

Can I? A part of me wants to tell him no, but I don't think I can, so I won't. I tentatively reach up, cupping his face. "I forgive you," is all I get out before his lips are on mine. The kiss starts off soft and sweet before becoming more and more urgent. My mouth opens, allowing his tongue inside. We do our familiar dance as his hands start moving down my body.

When Diego's hands reach my ass, he grabs me, lifting me until I'm sitting on the counter. Not once breaking the kiss, he spreads my legs and fits himself between them. My legs wrap around his waist, and he grinds his cock against me. "It's only been a week, but I've missed you," he mutters against my lips.

"I've missed you too." His hands slide up my thighs, and I lift my bottom up as he rips my panties away. I moan into his mouth as his fingers slide through my pussy.

"You're soaked," he growls. First one finger enters me and then another. I grip his hair as he pumps his digits in and out of me, moaning into his mouth. His fingers slide out of me and rub my clit before pushing back in. Diego does it over and over until I can't take it anymore.

"Please, make me come."

He pulls back, his eyes dark and hooded. "Please what, baby?"

My channel flutters around his digits. I open my eyes and look deep into his. "Please, Professor." His lips slam back down on mine, and he curves his fingers inside of me. He hits that glorious spot that makes my eyes roll back in my head. His other hand slides into my hair, and he grabs it at the base and yanks my head back.

"Let me hear you come, baby." He strokes that spot inside me while thumbing my clit. His teeth clamp onto the spot where my neck meets my shoulder, and I ignite. Crying out, I ride his fingers as he works me over and over until I collapse against his chest. A whimper escapes my lips as he pulls his fingers out of me, and I watch as he brings them to his lips, licking them clean.

He helps me off of the counter and kisses me as we walk blindly through my apartment. Until the back of my legs hit my bed and then I'm on my back and Diego is on top of me. It isn't long before we're both naked and he's driving his cock inside of me. I wrap my legs around his hips, and my back arches up off of the bed as I cry out. Together, we move in that familiar dance.

His gaze holds mine as he thrusts us both toward an orgasm. *"Te quiero mucho,"* he whispers as he reaches between us and begins to rub my clit. I feel that ache begin again and my cries become more urgent as I feel myself getting closer and closer to coming. "Please tell me you're close, baby."

"Yes," I moan. His head descends, and he wraps his lips around my nipple, sucking it deep. I swear that is all he needs to do, and I feel myself explode. My vision blurs, and my blood rushes in my ears. He pushes my legs up until I'm folded in half and begins pounding his cock into me with punishing thrusts until he plants himself to the root, groaning against my skin.

Diego lets my legs go, and they slide back down, wrapped around his hips. I hug him to my chest and let my fingers trail up and down his back. We stay like that until I feel him soften inside of me. He pulls out but switches us around so he's lying on his back and I'm up against his side with my head on his shoulder. His fingers trail softly up and down my back as I draw imaginary patterns on his chest.

"I love you," I whisper against the skin of his neck.

He presses his lips to my forehead. "I love you too, *mi espíritu libre hermoso.*" I feel my eyes get heavy and drift shut, and for the first time in a week, I go to bed happy.

***

Three weeks have gone by since Diego and I got back together. Things have been amazing between us. He's constantly making me smile or swoon, but it's been crazy busy too.

The night we got back together, I had woken up to something yummy smelling. I slipped on a nightgown and made my way out into the kitchen where I found Diego cooking something on the stovetop.

He smiled when he spotted me and held out his hand until I took it and let him pull me to him. "Did you sleep well, beautiful?"

"I did." I looked in the skillet and saw it was a grilled cheese. "Yum, that looks great."

"Good, because you're going to need your strength." A giggle bubbled up from my throat, and I kissed the underside of Diego's chin.

After we ate, we snuggled on the sofa and talked about the serious stuff. I didn't want to, but it was necessary. We decided we were going to Facetime with his parents so I could meet them virtually. As much as I wanted to say yes, I couldn't when Diego asked me to come home to Spain with him for winter break. My parents would be hurt, and I couldn't do that to them.

Vice versa for him as well. It would hurt his mom if he didn't come home, which I understood because he was so far away from them. It didn't matter, though. We were going to do things right this time. No secrets and no lying to each other or anyone else about our relationship.

I wasn't there, but when Diego went back to class, he brought a printed copy of the student/teacher relationship policy. Clint was looking all smug at him, so Diego slapped the papers on his desk and then told him to get the fuck out of his class. Clint did try to spread those pictures and videos of us around, but people didn't seem to care.

Oh sure, I got comments here and there, but for the most part, no one gave a shit what we did. Of course girls constantly came up to me, telling me how lucky I was. All I would tell them was, "Yes, I am."

Luckily, Clint vanished after that—he was probably hiding and licking his wounds. I know he met with the chancellor and withdrew from his classes for the rest of the semester, which worked just fine for me. I didn't want to see him at all.

That vile Penelope woman showed up last Friday night at Diego's while we were having dinner. He tried to get rid of her, and she was being a total bitch. I'd had it—I was tired of people trying to come between us. I marched outside and right past Diego until I stood right in front of her. "Listen, bitch! I don't know how much more clear he needs to be, but he does not want you."

"Who the fuck do you think you are? Why

would he want a fat bitch like you when he could have this?" She signaled to her body.

"Last time I checked, he liked *real* women, not Skeletor-looking bitches like you. How crazy and delusional are you? You had him followed? That's some crazy shit. You need to leave now before I lose my cool and beat your ass."

She looked around me to Diego. "Are you going to let her talk to me like this?"

"*Sí*. Now get the fuck out of here or I'll call the cops and have you picked up for harassment." Who knows what finally clicked in that bitch's head, but she finally got the picture.

"Fuck you both. You were a shitty fuck, anyway."

We watched her stomp down the steps and climb into her little sports car before peeling out like an idiot, and when she was finally gone, I let out the breath I was holding. Diego wrapped his arms around me. "That was amazing."

I turned my head to look at him. "I've never in my life done something like that." It was the truth. I'd always been a pacifist, the peacemaker in the family, but enough was enough. I was tired of people messing with us.

"Well, you could've fooled me. Is it bad to say that my dick is so hard right now?" He then threw me over his shoulder, took me inside, and showed me just how hard it was.

The one thing I've been dreading is calling my parents and letting them know that Diego and I are back together, but again I want to be honest and up front with everyone. Diego wanted to be there when

I made the call, but I didn't know if that was a good idea. We compromised; he'll be here but not in the room.

My dad is going to be the hard sell, so I decide to call him. "Hi, baby girl."

"Hey, Daddy. How are you?"

"I'm good, honey. What's going on?"

I take a deep breath. "I wanted to talk to you about something."

"You know you can talk to me about anything. What is it?"

"Diego and I are back together. Before you say anything, just know this: He broke up with me because he didn't want to come between us. He's a good man, Dad. I know he's older than I am and was my professor, but I withdrew from his class. Don't be mad—I'll be able to take it next semester with another professor." I tell him about Clint and how he tried to blackmail me and that it was Diego who went to the chancellor to turn him in and disclose our relationship. "Daddy, I know you're mad and disappointed in me, but I love him and he loves me."

Silence greets me from the other end, and I think for sure he'd hung up, but finally he sighs. "I'm not mad, and I'm not disappointed. He's not who I'd choose for my oldest daughter, but all we've ever wanted was for you to be happy. If he's who makes you happy, then that's all I could ever ask for, but I promise you that if he hurts you like he did, again, I will kick his ass."

I can't help the tears that begin to fall. "Thank you, Daddy."

"Baby girl, you, your sisters, and your mom are the best things that have ever happened to me. Your happiness is all I could ever hope for or want. I do expect you to bring him home the next time you're able so your uncles and I can welcome him into the brood properly."

I laugh, and it makes me feel hopeful. "Maybe he can come with me for spring break. He's going to Spain for winter break."

"I suppose that means we'll have to share you with Spain." I never thought of that. The idea of spending time in Spain makes me giddy...again, that's if he takes me.

"Yeah, maybe. I'm going to let you go, though. I'll see you in a couple of weeks. I love you, Dad."

"I love you too, sweetheart. No matter what, I love you. Oh, and your mom wanted me to tell you that Abby's having a little boy. Everyone is super excited for them."

"That's great. I'll have to call her and congratulate her, Ben, and Natalie."

We don't talk too much longer before hanging up. I step back inside Diego's home and find him in the living room watching soccer. He smiles at me when I step into the room. "Hey, baby, how'd it go?"

"It went really well. He expects me to bring you home for spring break. That's only if you want to come and I guess if we're even still together." I'm babbling.

He pulls me into his lap. "Oh, we'll still be together." I kiss his cheek and snuggle into him while he finishes watching the soccer match.

Life can't get much better than this, and I can't wait to see where this is going to go.

***

Diego

Two Months Later

I straighten my tie while looking at myself in the mirror. Tonight is the masquerade charity ball, and I can't wait to see Violet in her dress. She wouldn't let me see it before hand, but I'm sure she'll look gorgeous. My mom demanded that as soon as we were both ready that we send her pictures.

I had been worried about how she was going to act toward Violet, but after the first time they Facetimed, they seemed to hit it off. My mom is definitely a hard person to win over sometimes, but I think she could see that Violet is genuine. I think it also helped that my mom could see how happy she makes me. I hear my bedroom door open and turn my head. I'm struck speechless.

Violet is standing in front of me in a wine-colored dress. It's a silky-looking material that skims over her body and highlights her curves. The capped sleeves are a little off of the shoulder, and the front dips down just a little bit, showing off her cleavage. "Do I look okay?" She gives me a nervous smile. She's been freaking out about this since we'll be around a lot of faculty and not everyone has been cool with our relationship, but I've chosen to ignore them. We're not hurting anyone, and we love each other.

"Baby, you look so fucking beautiful right now. You take my breath away. Turn around. Let me see all of it." She smiles and slowly spins in a circle. The back of the dress dips down to right above her ass. "Fuck me. I'm going to be kicking some ass tonight."

"What? Why?"

"That dress, your makeup, and your hair." Which is up in a low chignon. "You're the whole package." She walks toward me and reaches up, adjusting my tie.

"You look pretty fine yourself. Who's to say I'm not going to have to kick some ass tonight too?" She grabs her clutch and wrap, and I lead her outside to my car. A month ago, she finally agreed to move in with me, and she sublet her apartment to Dani.

We park by the hall where the ball is happening, and there are people everywhere. Once we get out of the car, I tie Violet's mask on her. Instead of an elastic string, hers has a silk ribbon that matches the color of her dress, although the mask is black. I slip mine on and then escort her inside.

I know she notices some of the stares she's getting, but she ignores them. I'm pretty sure they're a mixture of curiosity, fascination, and jealousy. I hate that some of the other faculty wives and girlfriends have shunned her, but honestly whenever I look at Violet, I can see why they have. Not only is she physically gorgeous, but also her inner beauty far surpasses the physical. Everywhere we go, people are drawn to her and her infectious smile.

My hand rests on the small of her back, and the feel of her bare skin has me fighting a hard on. We're sitting with Chancellor Williams and his wife. They've been very good to us. He waves to us from our reserved table. We reach them, and I pull out Violet's chair for her. I sit her next to Tom's wife, Gloria. Tom stands up. "Let's go get some drinks."

After kissing Violet's cheek, I follow Tom to the bar. "Violet looks beautiful," he says. "Gloria said that she enjoyed shopping with her for that dress."

"I appreciate her taking Violet." We grab two glasses of champagne apiece and head back.

All night long, I can't take my eyes off of my girl. A smile always graces her lips. We eat, we dance, and walk around looking at all of the amazing silent auction gifts. There's one that Violet seems to keep looking at, and it's a trip to Barcelona. I wait until she's back at the table before I put in a bid. It's a big one—I hope to get it.

When I rejoin the table, I grab Violet to dance. Holding her close as we sway to the music is one of my most favorite things. "Are you having a good time?"

"Yes, I never went to my prom, so it's kind of cool that I get to experience it now…sort of. Thank you for bringing me."

"Absolutely, baby. I'm glad you're enjoying yourself." I cup her cheek in my hand. "You know we're going to spend the rest of our lives together, right?" She again gives me that breathtaking smile of hers.

"You're pretty confident in yourself, aren't you, Professor Torres?"

I kiss her thoroughly and then pull back. "Of course I am."

***

By the way, I did win that trip to Barcelona.

Epilogue

Violet

Three Years Later

I shift in my seat as I listen to the speeches. I can't believe I'm finally graduating. Last night was the wave goodbye party, and it was such a blast. Diego's parents came into town for everything as well as my grandma and mine.

These past three years have been amazing, hard, and wonderful all at the same time. The summer after Diego and I got back together, he took me to Spain, to Barcelona to be exact. The architecture was amazing, and every place we went, I'd tour as many of the structures as I could. We even spent a couple of days in Diego's hometown, and I finally got to meet his family. I loved them. They were a close family, and it was obvious how much they loved each other.

One thing I had noticed was they loved to feed me. I swear at one point I thought I was going to explode. They showed me around, and I got to see where Diego went to school, where he and his brother were born, and where his mom worked.

The night before we were due to fly home, Diego took me to this little restaurant on the Mediterranean Sea. After we ate, we walked along the water, and then he got down on his knee in front of me. He told me how much he loved me and how he couldn't imagine me not being in his life. He also told me that me walking into his class was the best day of his life. I tackled him right there in front of everyone, and of course I said yes.

We got married two years ago in New Orleans. All of our families were there for the small intimate ceremony and the huge party afterwards.

I look to the side and find my family sitting toward the bottom. Our fifteen-month-old daughter, Luciana, or Lucy, sits on her grandpa's lap, waving her chubby arms in the air. My dad catches my eye and winks at me. Lucy's birth was what caused me to get a bit behind in my classes. I should've graduated last year, but that's okay. I don't regret any of it.

When it's time, I line up with the other students. My hands tremble, and I don't know why I'm nervous—I've worked hard for this day. Then I hear it, and I smile. "Violet Renée Torres." I hear my mom and sisters screaming, and then I hear my beautiful little girl start calling for her mommy. I take my diploma, flip my tassel to the other side, and stop at the top of the stairs, smiling at my family again before heading back to my seat.

The rest of the ceremony is a blur, and then

they're dropping confetti from the ceiling and the jazz band starts to play. Since I don't know any of the other students that graduated with me today, I take off toward my family. Diego reaches me first, hugging me tightly to his chest. "I'm so proud of you, my beautiful wife."

"Thank you, my wonderful husband." With his arm around me, we head over to the rest of our family, and my mom starts taking tons of pictures.

My dad stops right in front of me with Lucy in his arms, but she immediately lunges for me. "Hi, my beautiful girl." Lucy looks like a combination of her daddy and me. She's got dark brown, curly hair, deep, soulful brown eyes, and a darker olive skin tone than me.

My dad wraps us both in his arms. "I'm so proud of you, honey. You worked so hard and have done such an amazing job."

My grandma comes to me next. "Your grandpa would be so proud of you." That brings tears to my eyes, but I know he would be. I just hate that Lucy will never meet her Great-grandpa Hutchins, but I'll always share my memories with her. "I wanted to tell you, too, that the house finally sold."

This makes me sad. I was hoping that my grandma would reconsider selling her home, but I get why she did it. Over the past year and a half, my dad and uncles had completely gutted and redid it, giving it a more modern look.

"That's great, Grandma. I hope whoever bought it creates some wonderful memories there." I hug her so she can't see my eyes fill with tears, but I quickly blink them away.

After the ceremony we all go out to eat, and then Diego, Lucy, and I head home so we can pack. We're driving to Beaufort where my family is throwing me a graduation party, and I can't wait to be surrounded by my loving family and all the babies that everyone seems to be spitting out.

***

Diego

We've been in Beaufort for a week, and I'm freaking out. About three months ago, I called Violet's dad and told him that I wanted to move to Beaufort. I want Violet and Luciana to be near family, and now that Violet's done with school, it's only natural that she begins working with her dad and uncles. After talking multiple times to Dustin, Dylan, and Luke, they've decided to expand their business, and Violet and I are going to work with them.

"Are you sure you want to give up teaching? Violet says how much you love it and that you're passionate about it," Dustin had said when I first brought it up.

"I love teaching, but I love Violet and Lucy more. I think I can bring a lot of fresh and new ideas to the table."

"Well, okay. We're excited to have you join us. I know Stacy will be tickled to have her daughter and grandbaby close."

After that, we got the ball rolling on a lot of stuff. Now I'm freaking because I did something without telling Violet, and I'm not sure how she's going to react.

"Where are we going?" she says from beside me. I blindfolded her so she has no clue what's happening. Lucy's with her grandparents getting spoiled rotten, I'm sure.

"Baby, it's a surprise."

We pull up in front of her grandparents' old house, which is now our house. When the idea to buy the house struck me, I called Violet's mom and talked to her about it. She was my biggest cheerleader about it and loved the idea of us moving closer to them.

I go to climb out. "Don't move, baby." Moving around the car, I help Violet out and then lead her up to the bottom of the steps. I smile when I see the huge red bow that Stacy put on the front door and the **"Welcome Home"** sign above it. "Okay, are you ready for your surprise?" She nods her head, hopping up and down.

Taking a deep breath, I slip the blindfold off, and she looks at the bow on the door and the sign above the door. She doesn't say anything for a long time, and I begin to think I made a mistake.

"You bought my grandparents' home? You bought this, for us?"

"Yes, baby. With Lucy and any more children we have, I wanted to be close to at least one set of grandparents. I know from the beginning you said your plan was to work with your dad and uncles, but what about your husband too?"

Tears fill her eyes. "You did this for us?"

"I did it for all of us, for you, me, and Lucy.

Should we take a look inside?" I use my key and open the door. She gasps as soon as we step inside. Her dad did a fantastic job updating the place and giving it a more modern look. They ripped up all of the carpet and laid down beautiful gray plank laminate flooring. I follow behind as she ooh's and aah's through every room.

The kitchen is all stainless steel appliances and granite countertops. The ceramic flooring matches the backsplash, giving it a unique look. We tour the rest of the house and then reach the master bedroom. Natural light pours in, giving it a soft look. A set of French doors opens up to a little terrace that looks out over the backyard. She peeks her head into the en suite and then turns back to me.

"This is the most amazing thing that anyone has ever done for me." She gets that look in her eye as she reaches behind her, unzipping her dress before letting it slip down her body to pool at her feet. Her curves are more pronounced, but fuck, her body is amazing.

"What are you doing, baby?"

"I want to christen our bedroom." With a growl, I back her up until she hits the wall.

I attack her mouth and then lick the seam of her lips until she opens to me. Our tongues duel as she unbuttons my pants and releases my cock that only she can get hard in seconds. I grunt into her mouth as she strokes it slowly. It doesn't take long before she has me ready to lose control. I rip her panties off, lift her leg, and then drive my cock deep inside her.

We move together, and her cries are music to my

ears. She is already starting to clamp down on my cock so I know she's getting close. When I reach out and pinch her nipple, she arches her back and moans. I keep driving deep into her, making sure to hit her clit each time until she clamps down on me, and she moans and cries as her orgasm detonates. I follow shortly behind her, coming deep inside her, bathing her walls with my cum. After we get our wits about us, I slowly pull out and then help her get dressed.

She wraps her arms around me after we're dressed. "Thank you for everything. I just have no words. You've made me so incredibly happy."

"Right back atcha, baby."

For someone who never thought he'd fall in love or get married, I can't imagine not having Violet in my life. She's giving me so much, and I hope that I can return the favor.

***

Nine months later, she gave me a beautiful son, Isaac Gary Torres, and I couldn't be happier.

The End

Unexpected Love

Book Four in the Love Stings Series

Chapter One

Joe

I take a sip of my beer while I watch my cousin/best friend, Violet, be danced around the floor by her new husband. Shit, I can't believe she's married. Hell, I can't believe she's married to someone twelve years older, but he makes her happy and seems like a good guy. As long as she's happy, I'll keep my trap shut.

I reach up and loosen up my tie—Violet's lucky. I love her and said yes when she asked me to be her Man of Honor. I figured she would've had one of her sisters or Abby or Carrington.

I'm only days older than her, and growing up, she and I were more like brother and sister than cousins. I feel someone standing next to me and turn to find my mom as she wraps her arms around my waist, so I wrap my arm around her shoulders.

"You look so handsome in your tux. It was a beautiful ceremony, wasn't it?"

"Thanks, Mom. Yeah it was, and it was the kind

1

I like—short and sweet." I bend down to kiss her forehead. My mom is a shorty, and I'm tall like my dad—hell, I'm taller than him now.

"That Chloe sure is a beautiful singer." Yes, she was, and there's nothing like fighting a hard-on standing up in front of a bunch of people, but shit, I've been fighting one since the first time I saw Chloe in a long time. It was after Violet's grandpa passed away and we were at her parents' house. I've never in my life had that kind of reaction to the opposite sex before. I had a body buzz to end all body buzzes, and I knew she felt it too, but I never got the chance to see if anything could happen. She went back to Atlanta before I could make a move.

"Yeah, she's great." My eyes scan the room, and I find her. She's with both of her dads' standing by the bar. Her hair is so dark it's almost black; her skin's like porcelain, but it's her eyes that truly suck me in. They're a cerulean blue and surrounded by dark lashes. I would've thought they were contacts, but her younger brother, Carter, has the same eyes. Chloe must feel my stare because she turns and looks right at me.

It gives me a thrill that even from across the room I see her cheeks turn a light shade of pink before she walks away from her parents. I don't know why, but she's been avoiding me all day. I know I can be a little intimidating. Since joining the police force, I've put on quite a bit of muscle and have tattoos on both arms. Add in my height and the shaved head, and it makes an intimidating package.

My mom kisses my cheek and then goes to my dad. My feet start carrying me toward Chloe when my nephew Dalton comes running toward me. "Hey, little man." I pick him up and kiss his chubby cheek.

He starts babbling in his secret toddler language that I don't understand at all. My eyes find her again, and she's watching us with a small smile on her lips. We head right to her, and this time she doesn't run. Of course she acknowledges little man first. "Hey buddy, aren't you just the cutest."

"Thanks," I tell her with a smirk.

"Haha. You're such a funny guy." Dalton squirms in my arms so I set him down, and he runs right to my mom. I shake my head because my parents spoil Abby's kids rotten, but I love it—I love how happy my sister is. It's hard to believe that it was so long ago that we almost lost Abby, but now's she's married with three kids and so incredibly happy. Her husband and I work together on the police force, and he's become a good friend.

I grab her hand. "Dance with me?"

She wants to say no, I can tell, but I don't give her the chance. I pull her out to the dance floor and begin swaying to the music. Her body feels so good pressed up against mine. In her heels she comes up to my nose, but without them I know she barely comes to my chin. Her tits are high and firm, and in the dress she's wearing, I'm getting a prime view of her cleavage. She's thin but soft, with enough curves highlighted in her silky blue dress to make my dick hard.

She smells like magnolias, and her skin is soft. "You look beautiful."

"You're not so bad yourself. The toast you gave

was really sweet."

"I don't think anything I've ever done has been classified as sweet." I pull her a little closer, not even caring that she can probably tell my cock's half hard, but it's her fault.

"Please, I saw you with your nephews earlier. They use you like their own personal jungle gym. You just smiled and let them do it. Last night during the rehearsal dinner, it wasn't lost on me that your niece sat with you and you guys were coloring for a while." Her pearly white smile puts an ache in my chest that is completely unfamiliar to me.

"It's nice to know that you've noticed me."

***

I strip out of my shirt and throw it on the chair in my hotel room. My brother wanted to share a room with me, but in the off chance I brought a woman back to my room, I told him to fuck off and to room with our cousin Luke. Unfortunately, I'm here alone with only the images of Chloe to keep me company. I could've gone to a bar to pick up a woman for the night, but I just didn't feel like it.

A knock on the door pulls me out of my thoughts. I look through the peephole and find the last person I expected to see on the other side of my door. When I open it, Chloe stands there in that fucking dress that turns me on like nothing else.

"Hey," she says.

"What are you doing here?" I stand back and watch her as she steps inside my room. Her sweet scent follows her in.

She stops in the middle of my room, and I let the door shut. Silence surrounds us, and I'm wondering what's happening. When Chloe finally turns around, she stuns me. She slips her dress off, and I watch in utter fascination as it slides down her delicious body. She saunters toward me until we're almost touching.

Her hands slide up my chest until they wind around my neck. "I want you to fuck me."

Acknowledgements

First and foremost, thank you to my husband, Jim, and my sons Ethan and (the real) Evan. Your never-ending support and encouragement means the world to me. You guys have shared this experience with me a hundred percent. Thank you for being understanding when dinner's late, the house isn't clean, and I'm behind on laundry, especially when I'm working on a deadline. Some days I don't know how I got so lucky to have the best male cheerleaders at my back.

Again, to my readers, who are always quick with encouraging words. I love their excitement when I share teasers, covers, or anything regarding my books.

To the whole Limitless team: editing, cover design, marketing, etc. You guys are wonderful to work with as always.

To all of the bloggers and friends I've met in the book industry: You all inspire me daily, and I can't wait until I meet a lot of you in person.

Last but certainly not least, to God because this ability to write is a gift I'll treasure forever.

About the Author

A Midwesterner and self-proclaimed nerd, Evan has been an avid reader most of her life, but five years ago got bit by the writing bug, and it quickly became her addiction, passion and therapy. When the voices in her head give it a rest, she can always be found with her e-reader in her hand. Some of her favorites include, Shayla Black, Jaci Burton, Madeline Sheehan and Jamie Mcguire. Evan finds a lot of her inspiration in music, so if you see her wearing her headphones you know she means business and is in the zone.

During the day Evan works for a large homecare agency and at night she's superwoman. She's a wife to Jim and a mom to Ethan and Evan, a cook, a tutor, a friend and a writer. How does she do it? She'll never tell.

Facebook:
https://www.facebook.com/pages/Evan-Grace/626268640762539

Twitter:
https://twitter.com/Evan76Grace

Website:
http://www.authorevangrace.com/

Goodreads:
https://www.goodreads.com/author/show/7788444.Evan_Grace